To Paula

School christmas party of
1961

ACHARN SCHOOL

Acharn
Primary
School

FOR THE WHITE COCKADE

FOR THE
WHITE COCKADE

by

ADMIRAL LORD MOUNTEVANS
K.C.B., D.S.O.

THE CHILDREN'S PRESS
LONDON AND GLASGOW

PRINTED IN GREAT BRITAIN

CONTENTS

CHAPTER I

THE GLEN OF THE SEVEN SIGNS

"Cam ye by Athol, lad wi' the philabeg,
  Doon by the Tummel or banks o' the Garry,
Saw ye my lad wi' his bonnet an' white cockade
  Leavin' his mountains to follow Prince Charlie?"

THE fading rays of the July sun were splintering themselves through the leafy branches of the trees of Glenfinnan as a shabbily-dressed lad paused in his ascent of the rocky glen and, seating himself on a moss-covered boulder, gave himself up to deep reflection.

One glance at the lad showed him to be a sturdily-built youth with laughing, blue eyes and a wealth of sandy-coloured hair that poked itself rebelliously from beneath his dusty bonnet to which—it may have been by chance, it may have been by destiny's dictates—he had fastened some sprigs of white heather.

His black velvet coat with its bright old silver buttons was slightly torn and looked soiled. The crumpled lace at his wrists and at his neck was grey rather than white and his kilt, of the Macdonald tartan, bore evidence of long wear.

"Oh, it's all wonderful here, Alastair, my lad," he said to himself. "And it helps you to forget that you were turned out of your father's house some days back to give place to your step-brother, but you have to remember that it's to be a fight in the world now, and unless the good Macdonald of Glenaladale takes kindly to your father's letter it's back you'll have to go to Lochavon and eat humble pie before your father's English son."

A wry smile flickered across the boy's face and then he sighed deeply and looked up towards the mountains, to remember the words of that sweet woman who had been his father's first wife.

"Never know defeat, Alastair Macdonald," she had said. "And you will never be defeated."

Alastair's mother had been dead for some years, but Alastair had never forgotten these words of hers.

As he sat there the whole sorry picture of what life had meant when she was gone came before the boy's eyes.

He pictured the day that Mrs. Harding and her son Saul had come to Lochavon; he saw again the little wedding between his father and the widow; and then he remembered all the bitterness that had come with her jealousy—perhaps he *had* resented her manner towards him and had shown his resentment in gloomy moods, but when he found Saul being put before him in his father's affections all the deep-red blood of the Macdonalds had come uppermost.

Alastair Macdonald, rising from the stone upon which he had been seated, put himself in an attitude of attack and then hit out at an imaginary enemy.

"And that is for your sneaking ways, Saul, and that for your lying tongue, and that because you're a Sassenach and that and that . . ." he cried.

Alastair struck out at the air, but each blow reminded him of that fight with his step-brother which had been the reason of the split between Alastair Macdonald and his father.

"You'll go to my cousin at Glenaladale," the elder Macdonald had said grimly. "I am sick and tired of your behaviour here, Alastair."

At that moment Alastair had said nothing. Standing by his father's desk he had watched the letter written and then, when it had been sanded, had taken it without a word and with a switch of his kilt had walked from the house without even a farewell to his step-mother.

There was one living soul at Lochavon, however, whom Alastair did mean to say farewell to, and that was old Kenneth Macdonald, Kenneth who was supposed to be mad and who depended on the Laird's charity for his food and shelter, although Hamish Macdonald, Alastair's father, had never been known as generous in this respect.

Alastair had searched high and low for Kenneth, his poorer kinsman, and had found the old man seated by the burn nigh to the little cottage where he lived, and Alastair had told him what had happened—why he was going away.

Kenneth had gripped the lad's hand and, looking mysteriously at his young master, had smiled.

"It's the note that is calling Alastair, ' core of my heart,'" he had said. "And the deep roll of the drum. I heard it here by the burn last evening and it led me over the hill, the call is coming to the true Macdonald. You'll be going to wait for him—to be ready for his coming maybe, young Laird. The seven signs shall lead you—look for the seven signs. He will not be long now—please Heaven it be in my time!"

The words had deeply mystified the boy, but *there*, Kenneth's words generally did, so Alastair had put them down to the old man's dreams and had then set off. He had seen Kenneth waving a last good-bye to him, and at the bend in the road he had forgotten his poorer kinsman's strange phrases and now the shades of Glen Finnan shrouded the young Macdonald in.

"Ah, well," he exclaimed at last. "Small use staying here and mooning. I must find some shelter for the night for I cannot possibly be with the Macdonald until midday to-morrow."

Picking up the small bundle which he had been carrying, and which comprised most of his worldly wealth, including a few gold coins his father, a mean man, had given him before his departure, Alastair began his upward tramp as the shadows lengthened beneath the trees.

He had gone but a few paces when, from the crags above him, there sounded the deep-throated note of a reed pipe.

Alastair paused and listened intently, for there was no soul in sight; and now that call had been taken up lower

down the glen. Alastair heard it winging away in the
distance and the echoes of other pipes that had picked up the
haunting note came to him.

"A signal."

It was getting quite dark now and he looked about him
apprehensively.

But nothing came from the approaching night save the
sighing of the wind down the glen, so, easier in mind, he
trudged upwards. He took the precaution, however, to
loosen the claymore in its scabbard . . .

Suddenly, as he mounted the glen, stumbling over the
boulders that gave to the way the semblance of a road, a
ray of light on his left hand side and some little way above
him attracted his notice, so that he paused.

Alastair's eyes lit up with relief. The light would be
coming no doubt from a cottage or a hut on the glen side,
and that would mean that his wearisome journey was to
end, for that night at any rate.

Turning away from the path he clambered over the rocks
and mounted the steeps of the glen until at last he saw,
silhouetted against the deep blue of the night sky and the
white stars, the shape of a hut.

It was something of a climb, but Alastair, born and bred
amidst the mountains, hurried like a chamois from rock
to rock.

Once he had to scale a part that was almost precipitous,
but, with the help of his claymore and his dagger, he reached
the summit at last and found himself on the threshold of
a little hut, with the light from it throwing him into bold
relief.

Then, as he stood there, in the rays of the candle-light,
there came to his ears the rasping sound of steel against
stone—and then Alastair saw!

Bending over a grindstone which he was working with
his feet was a white-bearded old man, but old as he was his
kilted frame was the frame of a giant, and his large sinewy
arms were holding a great sword from which the sparks

flew as the stone gave it the edge the old Highlander was seeking.

For some little time he stood there, waited until the sword-worker had finished and the grindstone ceased to revolve—then Alastair stepped forward and came into the hut.

Like a panther the old man turned, and before Alastair knew what had happened two steel-strong hands were about his throat.

"Who comes here so late and on what errand? Speak quickly or it's a dead man ye'll be."

Alastair found it difficult to speak, for already those fingers were tight about his neck, but he managed to force a laugh.

"An honest traveller," he said. "A Macdonald carrying a message to the Macdonald of Glenaladale."

The old Highlander loosened his grip and looked at Alastair with a searching gaze, and the few glances satisfied him.

"Come in," he said gruffly, and with that he closed the door and took another look at his visitor.

"You travel late, Macdonald," he said. "Why came ye here when the road lies below?"

"I was tired out," answered Alastair, "and saw your light so I climbed to it hoping that you would give me shelter for the night."

For some moments the old man did not speak. He was taking careful stock of Alastair. At last a smile flickered across the rugged features.

"Ye're weel-faured, callant," he said. "You shall stay here the night and in the morning I'll sharpen that claymore of yours. I've sharpened many of late, fine swords some of them, but it is not always the sword—not always the sword, laddie, as ye ken—it is this that lies behind it."

The old man bent his arms until the muscles stood out like knots as the hand closed over the great hilt of the broadsword with the razor-like edge.

Somehow, at that moment, there came to Alastair a thought of old Kenneth Macdonald. He could not understand why, but it seemed that what the old man had said at parting had a deeper significance now than it had had then.

"So the light drew you to Mackenzie's shieling, did it?" said the old man. "Now tell me, lad, about your life and who your father might be—and your mother. Perhaps you are English on your mother's side, maybe she's proud of the Hanoverian."

All these things Alastair stoutly denied, and realising that Mackenzie demanded frankness he told him everything that he knew of his home and found that he won a deep sympathy from the old Highlander for so doing.

Mackenzie fed him and made him a bed of rushes for the night, and with the morning he sharpened Alastair's sword as he had promised and walked some way on the road with his guest, having first resolutely refused the small coin that Alastair had offered him.

"There's your way now," he said. "And God speed, lad, and be ready . . ."

With this cryptic remark he turned and walked back the way he had come, leaving Alastair to descend to the glen and resume his journey.

Alastair felt refreshed and invigorated by the morning air as he swung along with a song on his lips, and he was still singing when he came upon a silent figure lying concealed behind a rock.

It was the body of a man.

With a cry of dismay Alastair knelt down at the man's side and placed his hand over the man's heart and bent his head to listen for any sounds of life.

The man was dead and the dirk in his back told how he had died.

Alastair had known but little of death, and this horror, with which he had come face to face so suddenly, sent the blood draining from his cheeks.

Bending over the figure he ran his hands through the dead man's pockets. They were empty, all save one, and in that one there was just a scrappy piece of crumpled paper which had evidently escaped some previous searcher's notice.

It was only a short note and this is how it ran:

" *Find out all you can—we believe it is a rumour. There would be no attack from the North, since France, so our agents inform us, has refused her aid. Keep in touch with M. at Edinburgh: he will advise you.*"

It was mystifying to Alastair—very mystifying.

There was nothing he could do save mark the spot and come later with others to give the man Christian burial, so, doffing his bonnet, and bending his head to utter a short prayer, Alastair took the road again.

It was half an hour later that he came to an aisle of trees and, to Alastair's amazement, he saw that some hand had been at work in disfiguring them, for, on every third tree to both sides of him, there was a deep gash in the bark.

He could not but think deeply now of all these strange happenings in this glen which was so much a picture of peace and yet held so much mystery—and yes, death! What did, what could, it all mean?

Mackenzie had given Alastair some food for his midday meal, and at last he, the lad, felt that it was about time he ate it, for he had breakfasted early and the pangs of hunger were beginning to make themselves felt.

Leaving the road, he walked through the trees and, finding a little glade, lay down amid the bracken and began to munch his piece of bread and meat.

The sun was hot above him, and Alastair, finishing his meal, and finding the fresh bracken most amazingly comfortable, lay back and was soon asleep.

For some little time he slept, and it was a strange sound that stirred him, the sound of a deep shout.

Very cautiously he raised himself and peered through the fronds of the bracken to see a sight that amazed him.

The glade was robbed of all its peace now, for in the centre of it was a gathering of kilted and armed men whose claymores clashed on their targets as they raised a lusty shout.

They were surrounding a tree stump upon which a tall, white-haired old man was standing. *The man was Mackenzie.*

Alastair realised now that he was in a very uncomfortable position. Mackenzie had shown plainly the previous night that he had a quick way with eavesdroppers, and, although he had convinced him last night that he was not playing the spy, Alastair realised now that Mackenzie would have every reason for suspecting him for this second incident.

With the stealth of an Indian, Alastair crept back through the bracken, watching the men in the glade as he crawled away, and, when he came to the road, he ran as hard as he could, so that he could place a safe distance between himself and that strange gathering of Highlanders.

On up the glen he went until the way opened out and the rocks gave place to gentle slopes and green fields. Here there were biggins, and at the doorway of one of them a woman was standing. As Alastair passed she raised her eyes, and the boy saw that they were wet with tears.

He doffed his bonnet and she beckoned him.

"So it's true," she whispered, glancing at his bright claymore. "They all be going and a wee callant like yersel will no be left out. It's brave we must all be when the wee laddies go. God speed ye, bonnie lad."

With that she turned and walked wearily back towards the biggin just as the door opened and a young girl appeared in the opening.

Her eyes were alight with joy, and something had given her an added colour: perhaps it was the new tartan shawl and kilt she was wearing.

It was of the Stuart tartan.

Alastair eyed it with surprise—he knew the tartan well, and so did every Highlander.

The Stuart plaid sent a quickening pulse in his heart, and standing there he suddenly remembered what old Kenneth had said, "The Seven Signs shall lead you—look for the seven signs."

They had called Kenneth mad, but now Alastair knew that his gift was something other than madness. The pipes, the sharpening of the claymore, the dead man, the cut trees, the mysterious gathering, the weeping woman and now the girl in the Stuart plaid.

The seven signs, and, with this seventh, he understood.

"Prince Charlie," he whispered. "Prince Charlie is coming!"

CHAPTER II

"RED ANGUS"

THE man was writing—writing as though very life itself depended upon the quick dispatch of the work he had in hand.

Once the writer paused, and laid down his pen, as though some sudden thought had made him alter his purpose, but then he picked the quill up again and swept the lace at his sleeves aside and bent over the new letter that he was writing and, so it appeared, he found it more difficult to write than the others that had gone before it.

Macdonald of Glenaladale yawned wearily and sat back in his chair and clapped his hands. The curtains at the far end of the long room were thrown aside and a very tall Highlander passed by them and stood there respectful and attentive.

"Ask M. de Valerau to come in, Angus," he said, somewhat wearily.

The Highlander withdrew, and in a few moments had returned with a faultlessly dressed individual who, as he passed the curtains, bowed low.

The newcomer was clad in a black satin suit and wore a white wig, perfectly set and tied with a neat satin bow at the back, whilst a small black patch on his left cheek stood out boldly against the dead white of his thin, sharply-cut face.

With his left hand on his sword hilt and his right to his heart he bowed profoundly to the Macdonald of Glenaladale, and the Macdonald rose and bowed in response.

"From over the water?"

Macdonald glanced keenly at his visitor and drew a chair forward for the Vicomte de Valerau.

"So France has refused her aid?" he murmured.

An expression of deep pity lay in the Vicomte's eyes—a look full of sincerity.

"I did my utmost," he said. "But what would you have? England, we know, suffered a severe defeat at Fontenoy, but still our war drags on and the people murmur. It was suggested to His Majesty that Marshal Saxe should lead an expedition, but it would be perilous to France to risk his loss or the loss of men when new armies are being formed against us."

Macdonald nodded.

"So we must abandon all hope of help?"

"Alas, but I fear so," said the Vicomte. "I used my best offices in a cause that has always been near to my heart. Feeling for you, I sorrow myself."

Macdonald turned in his chair and his gaze was stern.

"Tell me of our Prince," he said quickly. "We have had but poor reports. Is the cause his life, or has exile lulled the desire to raise the Stuart standard?"

A flush mantled the face of the Vicomte.

"It is all he lives for," he answered at once. "I served with him the Spanish wars, and then, as a mere boy of fifteen, receiving his baptism of fire, he always spoke to me of the great dream. You know what his uncle, the Marshal Berwick, said to him?"

"He spoke well of His Royal Highness," said Macdonald. "I thank you, M. le Vicomte. You have given me encouragement to continue with this matter. We Jacobites, loyal to an old cause, have pondered gravely on the return of Prince Charles Edward, but God knows there will be no want of claymores to support him when he does come."

De Valerau smiled.

"And many rapiers as well, Monsieur," he said quietly. "I have come to the standard in the name of those in France who love your Prince."

Macdonald's hand shot out and gripped that of the Frenchman.

"Then we shall meet again," he said. "Until then, Monsieur, *au revoir*."

The Vicomte bowed and withdrew, ushered out by Angus Macdonald, the Highlander, a tower of strength and a monument of silence.

For a few moments Macdonald sat back in his chair.

"Angus!" he called at last. "Come here, Angus."

"France refuses aid," said Macdonald of Glenaladale sharply. "The moment has come, 'Red Angus,' when we shall have to stand or fall alone. Has Clanranald's messenger come yet?"

"No," came the answer. "Nor Boisdale's."

"They tarry over long," said Glenaladale impatiently. "I cannot stand this tension, Angus—waiting for news is the worst part of the battle. Has no one arrived?"

A smile flickered across the firm face of "Red Angus," and he looked at his claymore and laughed lightly.

"Our forces grow larger," he said, in his deep and resounding voice. "But a few minutes since a lad arrived; ragged he is, and wearing a sprig of white heather, and his name is the name we bear. He told me his claymore was sharp and he came about the Prince's business."

"A Macdonald, say you?" murmured Glenaladale. "A Macdonald of where?"

"He tells me he bears a letter from a distant kinsman, Macdonald of Lochavon," said Angus, back to his grave demeanour again.

A frown crossed Glenaladale's face.

"Hamish Macdonald," he muttered. "We were never friends, and he brings a lady of the Hanoverian bedchamber back to Scotland as his bride—how should this lad come about the Prince's business?"

"I'll see the lad," said Macdonald of Glenaladale at last. "Bring him here at once, Angus."

Angus strode away and, in the outer room, found Alastair looking in wonderment at a box filled with white favours.

Alastair had not heard the Highlander coming, and Angus paused to watch the Chief's visitor.

Alastair bent over the box and, picking out one of the cockades, unpinned the white heather from his bonnet and then replaced both the heather and the cockade where only the heather had been.

It was then that Angus coughed discreetly. Alastair swung round, saw Macdonald's henchman, and flushed a ruddy red.

"Glenaladale will see ye," said Angus gruffly. "Come this way."

Feeling not a little shamefaced and holding in his hand his bonnet with its white cockade, Alastair followed Angus into the long room where waited Macdonald of Glenaladale.

Alastair's first glance at the kinsman of his father told the boy that here was a firm and resolute character; not a little awe-inspiring, in fact, for Macdonald's gaze was by no means kindly.

"Well," he said sharply. "What seeks a son of Lochavon with the Macdonald of Glenaladale."

Alastair searched in his pockets for the letter his father had written, and finally managed to find the precious billet, which, with an attempt at a bow, he handed to the stern man who was looking down at him.

Macdonald of Glenaladale just glanced at the letter. If he had expected a eulogy of the boy he was interviewing he was very much mistaken, for Lochavon had been sparing in praise of his own son.

"What do you want me to do for you?" he asked. "Was there not room for you in your father's house?"

Alastair lowered his head to conceal the pain that had crept into his eyes at that harsh utterance, then he raised his head proudly.

"When I set out I fancied that I might find employment in *your* service," he said boldly. "I have abandoned that idea now, as I wish for employment in a better cause . . ."

"A better cause," murmured the Chief. "What cause?"

"The cause of Prince Charles," said Alastair quietly.

A sarcastic smile came across the lips of the Macdonald of Glenaladale.

"But I am not for him," he said softly, watching the impression his words made on the boy. "I am not one to take up lost causes. The Jacobites are my best enemies."

The blood drained from Alastair's face. It suddenly occurred to him that perhaps he had betrayed a secret.

The next moment his claymore flashed out, and with a cry he dashed towards the Laird.

"Draw then, traitor to the clan!" he cried. "Have at you, for I am for Prince Charles!"

If it had not been for the quick action of Angus things might have gone badly with the Macdonald of Glenaladale and some of the history of Scotland altered.

Angus sprang between the lad and the Laird, and his own claymore, broad of blade and flashing in the light that came through the mullioned windows, rasped on Alastair's.

Ring of steel upon steel in an echoing room with a stern man leaning back against an oaken table, with a gay smile on his lips as he watched the sword play!

Alastair's sharp attack had driven Angus into the centre

of the room, but now the broad sword of the big Highlander was answering stroke with stroke.

Clash of steel on target and the merry music of the sword, with a laugh in the eyes of Angus, and not a little admiration, as this young cockchafer sought to cut down his guard and win the day.

It happened very suddenly. Just a downward stroke and a pain in Alastair's wrist, and his claymore fell, a harmless thing, on the floor at his feet.

"Pierce me!" he said defiantly, as Angus lowered his claymore. "If all are against Prince Charles what is there left?"

" A commission in his service," said a soft voice, and, as Alastair turned to see who had spoken, Macdonald of Glenaladale, with a glad cry on his lips, ran to where a man stood in the opening between the hanging curtains.

"Clanranald!" he cried. "What news, Clanranald?"

CHAPTER III

CLANRANALD'S COMMISSION

ALASTAIR'S first thought had been that this newcomer would prove to be some ally, come to aid him in his defence of the young Chevalier, Charles Edward, but, when he saw Glenaladale gripping both Clanranald's hands and begging for news, the young Macdonald felt that either the speaker had spoken falsely or that there was something here that was too deep for a simple lad's mind to solve.

No sooner had Glenaladale cried, "What news, Clanranald?" than Clanranald answered, "He comes."

The next moment the two walked back into the room with the surprised eyes of a boy glancing from them to where his useless claymore lay, far out of instant reach.

"Red Angus," who had perceived what lay in Alastair's

mind, moved quietly towards the claymore, picked it up, and, with a light laugh, extended it, hilt foremost, to the lad he had fought with but recently.

"You will need it," he said softly, as with amaze Alastair took the blade, nor was there any animosity in the Highlander's look.

Alastair raised his head proudly and looked full at Clanranald.

"If you are for Prince Charles, sir," he said, "you little know the value of *this* Macdonald's loyalty."

Glenaladale did not speak; instead he came towards Alastair and laid both his hands on the boy's shoulders.

"Alastair Macdonald," he said gravely, "in these times one has to pick out the friends from the enemies, and oftentimes it is no easy matter. It is also a good thing to know a man's mettle."

He paused.

"My kinsman, Clanranald here," he said at last, "will tell you that there is no more fervent Jacobite than Macdonald of Glenaladale; no man more keen in loyalty to Prince Charles, no man more anxious to give his life if need be, so that the Stuart may come back into his own."

Alastair's clouded brain began to get clear.

"So it was a trick?" he said quickly. "The fight . . ."

"It was a test, lad," said Glenaladale at once, "and one in which you gave every proof of your desire to serve the Prince. You may consider yourself in my service."

He moved away, having first shaken his young kinsman's hands, and Alastair was just following Angus when Clanranald laid his hand lightly on Glenaladale's arm.

"You forget that I gave the lad his commission," he said gaily. "But serve you he shall when first he has served me, for already I have work for him."

"Angus," he added, "see to your charge, and with as much haste as possible. I have an urgent matter to get settled and our young giant-killer here seems peculiarly suited for the work."

Just a little shamefaced at having been so well deceived, Alastair followed Angus out of another door from the one by which he had come into the room and down a short flight of steps into a small room that looked a veritable armoury.

The boy's eyes lit up with pleasure and excitement as he saw the swords, rapiers, claymores, targes, bucklers and daggers that rested on the walls, to say nothing of the stacked muskets and pistolets.

Angus was the picture of solemnity, and now, as Alastair looked at him, he shook his head.

"You're a puir swordsman on the defence, wee laddie," he said, "although when you attacked me first I was thinking that it would be no place by the Laird's side that I would fill in the day of battle. Ye have a remarkable spirit, but ye will have to strengthen that guard or it is small use you'll be to Prince Charlie or any other body."

Angus laid his strong right hand on Alastair's hair and forced the boy's head back.

"I'll say this for you, callant," he said in his deep tones, "you were a man to come at Angus as ye did, and Angus likes you for it, and I'm your kinsman as well, so there's my hand of friendship on this happy meeting."

Alastair flushed with pleasure, and the next moment his hand was in that of the big Highlander, and he knew that he had found a friend indeed.

"Now," said Angus, "the Chief is most particular about neatness of dress and discipline, so I'll find you a new doublet and a buckle for your shoon."

"That doublet would be unworthy of the service, the great service you'll be going out on for Clanranald, but it's a problem to find another at so short a notice . . ."

Angus thought for a moment and then a light shone in his eyes and he walked quickly towards a cupboard, threw it open, and revealed a black box, which he lifted from the cupboard and laid on the floor.

"It occurs to me," he said, "that it is time to have done

with relics of Prince Charlie, now that he is coming himself to get back his own throne which those sneaking thieves stole from his kinsman."

Angus had uncorded the box and, with a dramatic lift of the box lid, he revealed a little black velvet coat with small silver buttons and fragile-looking lace at the sleeves.

"This was brought from France," he said softly, "by one of the Prince's old retainers. It was brought for me and here for many a year I have kept it, so that there should be something of Prince Charlie's in this part of Scotland. Often, when I have thought that maybe he would never return to his own, I have come here to see the coat and the little silk bonnet and I have been given renewed courage."

"How you must value it, Angus!" said Alastair. "But see, there is a hole, in the sleeve there," added the boy, pointing to a neat hole in the velvet.

"Aye, there's a hole there," said Angus. "A hole that was never mended because it told me that our laddie was a brave laddie, and that in battle, fighting against the Spaniards, the bullet pierced the sleeve there when he was leading men to the attack. It's a gallant little coat."

"Strip off your old tunic, laddie," he said quickly.

Alastair drew back.

"You don't mean . . ." he began; but Angus interrupted him.

"Strip it off," he ordered. "It's this coat that ye'll wear, and ye'll not disgrace the coat for you're a brave laddie yersel and ye'll always remember that it belonged to Prince Charlie."

Alastair slipped the coat on and then Angus buttoned it and saw that everything set properly over the kilt.

Seated on an upturned drum the great Highlander surveyed his charge from every possible angle.

"You look gay, laddie," said the Highlander, satisfied at last that the buckles of Alastair's shoes were bright enough and that the bonnet was at the right angle.

"And the cockade?" asked Alastair, feeling that it was

something of a responsibility in addition to a great honour, to wear what had once been worn by Prince Charles Edward.

"On the bonnet with it," said Angus. "You won't be alone in wearing *that* favour."

So interested had the two been in their work of making Alastair look like a bright new pin that they had not heard the sound of feet on the stairs, but at last Alastair turned and saw the grave eyes of Clanranald looking down at him, but they were not so grave as usual as they gazed at this merry-faced boy with jaunty bonnet and rakish claymore.

"What is your Christian name, Macdonald?" he asked with quiet dignity.

"Alastair!" came the instant reply.

"Can you ride, Alastair?"

"I have often ridden, sir," said Alastair respectfully.

"Then come with me now, and let us discuss the work I want you to do—that is," he added with a little laugh, "if Angus is thoroughly satisfied that you do credit to the Glenaladale Macdonalds."

Clanranald turned on his heel and Alastair, with a wave of the hand to Angus, ran up the old stone steps and so came to Glenaladale's library.

"Alastair," said Clanranald. "I have reason to believe that His Royal Highness the Prince will land first on the Island of Erisca. There is some doubt about the kind of following he will get when the news becomes known that he means to make a bid for the throne."

Clanranald paused to let his words sink deeply into the lad's mind.

"You will go to Erisca," he said, "and the moment that Prince Charles lands you will come post-haste back here."

A grave look came over Clanranald's rugged face.

"Do not think," he said, "that all will be friends you meet on your way. There are spies about, and those who are evilly disposed towards Prince Charles. Keep your own counsel—and these letters," he added. "One you will hand to the Laird of Kinlochmoidart, the other is for my kinsman, the elder Clanranald. See that they are delivered to each of these gentlemen in person, and see to it that when this is done you make at once for the coast and so across to the Island of Erisca and there wait. I rely upon you, Alastair Macdonald, to be true to the trust I have in you and watch for Prince Charlie's coming."

"I *will* be true to that trust," said Alastair. "My life is at Prince Charlie's service."

"Then good-bye, and God-speed, lad," said Clanranald. "Now get ye off to bed, for you have a dangerous mission before you and you will want all your wits for the work. I shall be leaving at midnight, so we shall not meet for some little time, for I have far to go through the night on another mission for the cause."

They gripped hands, and then Alastair returned to Angus, who showed him to the room that had been prepared for him by Duncan, Glenaladale's oldest henchman.

.   .   .   .

When Alastair awoke Clanranald was far on his journey northwards, and Glenaladale had put many a mile between himself and his home.

"They rode away together, laddie," said Angus, as he watched Alastair eat the porridge that Duncan had prepared for him.

"But they took different roads," added Angus. "One rides north, the other south, and soon you will be riding too—the horse is waiting for ye now."

Alastair's eyes lit up with delight as he saw the animal —he had seen but had never ridden so fine a mount as this, and he told Angus so.

"You're on important work, laddie," said the gaunt Highlander, "and you must look important."

"I shan't ride with too light a heart, Angus," Alastair said. "This is a heavy responsibility and I am not afraid of the danger so much as making a failure of my first commission."

Angus helped Alastair into the saddle and, looking up at him, laughed.

"You've got the true Macdonald caution, laddie," he said. "It doesn't do to be over-sure of yourself ever, and you ride with the right spirit—do your best, no man can do more than that. Be careful of that guard of yours, if it comes to a fight, laddie. And now Godspeed and remember it is for Prince Charlie."

"I will," came the reply, and, bending over, the boy shook "Red Angus" by the hand and the next moment, turning his horse's head, cantered off down the glen.

He was riding for Prince Charlie, and, if it was a dangerous adventure, it was also a gay one.

CHAPTER IV

THE STORM

ALASTAIR did not go direct to the mainland and then to the Island of Erisca, for his messages took him far afield.

When he delivered the letter to Kinlochmoidart the Laird gave him another letter to take, explaining that this instruction was in Clanranald's letter to him.

Three days went by, days of hard riding and but little rest, for Alastair was all anxiety to finish this matter of messenger work and get to the Island to wait for Prince Charles.

Kinlochmoidart's mission had sent him a long way out of his course, but at last the day arrived when there was only the letter to the elder Clanranald to be delivered, and Alastair marked the look of disfavour with which Clanranald's kinsman received the billet.

The elder Clanranald had no missive to send, so, with a free mind, Alastair, after a meal, mounted his fed and rested horse and set out for the real task that Clanranald the younger had set him.

Alastair was riding through very wild country, and he found few places where he could beg hospitality.

He had been gone but six hours from his last halt—the hut of a chair-maker in the forest—when suddenly his roan horse reared up in the air and then fell forward, throwing Alastair heavily to the ground.

The fall must have stunned the lad, for when Alastair came to, it was to find that night had fallen and that the rain was pelting down in torrents, and near at hand lay the roan.

With a pain in his left leg Alastair rose to his feet and walked towards the faithful animal, to find, to his dismay, that the roan was dead.

There was nothing for it but to push on without a mount, but before Alastair left the faithful old beast he bent over and kissed the cold, soft muzzle of the roan, and then, taking the cloak from the back of his now useless saddle, he slipped it about his shoulders and hurried on through the storm.

For half an hour he tramped through the trees with the great flashes giving him an occasional clue as to his bearings, and at last, in the glare of the lightning, he saw that he had come to the edge of the forest and that a gentle slope led down to a rocky shore.

"The sea!" he exclaimed.

To his left was the light of a fishing village, and he knew that somewhere out there, set in the sea, was the Island of Erisca, and near at hand was a boat, rocking on the rising waves.

Slipping his shoes and stockings off, and taking off his kilt and throwing it over his shoulders, Alastair waded out to the boat and clambered into her, to find that she was a sailing yawl. The mast and sail lay stowed away in her bottom.

Working with quick, eager fingers he raised the mast and

set the sail and then drew up the little anchor that held her fast.

The next moment his tiny craft was bounding out across the waves, as the storm grew more angry and the roll of thunder deepened across the waters.

Looking before him, he saw that the rollers were raising white, menacing heads at him, and behind him there were no longer any lights to show where the village lay.

It seemed hours that he sailed outwards with the wind, ever and anon nearly capsizing his frail craft.

She was shipping seas now and, in the glare of the lightning Alastair could see how deep the water was in the little boat.

It was at this moment—just when he believed that he had gone right out of his course and that both himself and his craft were lost, that he saw two red lights quite near at hand.

In the sudden fall of the wind he heard the flapping of slackening sail and then his boat grazed against the side of a ship.

Alastair, with the water above his ankles now, stood up in his sinking boat.

"Help!" he cried. "Help!"

A lantern glowed above him and in its light Alastair saw a keen, handsome face.

Above the lad there sounded the patter of bare feet on the rainswept deck.

"What is it, your Royal Highness?" cried a rough voice through the night.

The next thing that Alastair knew was that, with a heart full of thankfulness, he was grasping a rope.

CHAPTER V

COUNCILS OF WAR

"The news frae Moidart cam yestreen
Will soon gar mony ferlie,
For ships o' war ha'e just come in
An' landed Royal Charlie."

IN the blackness of the night the gleam of a ship's lantern, falling on his face, almost blinded Alastair as, hand over hand, he pulled himself up the rope and was able at last to swing his leg over the ship's rail whilst willing hands helped him to the vessel's deck.

The next moment a great hand gripped Alastair's shoulder and, past the light of the lantern, he saw two dark eyes looking into his own.

"It's a lad, your Royal Highness!" said a gruff voice. "A mere lad, but what he was doing in that sea is a mystery."

As Alastair heard those words, and now that the fear of death had passed, a great feeling of relief came to him—and understanding as well.

Behind the man who held the lantern, in the shadows beneath the mainmast, a slim figure was standing, a kilted figure who now came forward and stood in the red circle of light cast by the big lantern.

The man was tall and wore a plain black coat with a white shirt beneath it and a cambric stock fixed by a small silver buckle. He wore a fair wig, and his eyes seemed filled with smiles as they looked at the lad who had been so miraculously saved from the sea.

There was no mistaking his manner. Here was a man to be followed, a man of dignity, a man who had been called "your Royal Highness."

As Alastair gazed at him, saw the frank look and the

simple clothes that were not a little pathetic in their simplicity, he bent his knee and caught at the young man' hand, and bowing his head touched the hand with his lips

"It is no mystery, your Highness," said Alastair. "It i the grace of God that I should be the first Macdonald t welcome you back to your own."

"Loose him, O'Sullivan," said a softly modulated an musical voice. "Here is no spy or enemy. If this be th first omen pray God I have many such, for it must be good one when a Macdonald cub comes to tell of the ram pant lions. Look at me, lad."

Alastair sprang to his feet, and the heavy hand of Captai O'Sullivan no longer gripped the boy's shoulder.

O'Sullivan stood aside as from below there came th sound of feet, and the next moment three gentlemen cam running forward, to pause as they saw the strange sight o a sea-wet lad standing erect whilst the hands of Princ Charles Edward rested on his shoulders.

"I am indeed your Prince," he said softly, "and this shi is the *Doutelle*, out of the Loire. We are bound for Erisca but the storm has driven us out of our course. From whon do you come and whither were you bound, lad?"

"The mission was for the Laird of Clanranald," sai Alastair simply. "I came to wait for your Royal Highness rode through the night and chanced to find a boat."

Charles Edward turned towards the three gentlemen who were looking with interested eyes at Alastair.

"Came through the night and through that sea, gentle men," he said softly. "Came to wait for me, and would no be denied by the storm. Could ever exile have such welcome, could there ever be such a sign to lead our caus through the darkness! Athol, Sheridan, Strickland, O'Sul livan, we come to our home in tempest to find the young heart of Scotland rising from the waves to bid us welcome!'

There was a light of fierce exultation in the eyes and Charlie's hands trembled with some strange fervour.

"Athol," said Prince Charles Edward, "I give this laddi

nto your care. See that he is well served and prepare him
for the duties he will perform when we make Erisca."

With that, and chatting to Captain O'Sullivan, his trusted
adjutant, Prince Charles walked forward.

Alastair saw that the Duke of Athol was all anxiety to
question him.

"What have you seen?" he asked quickly.

A smile came into Alastair's eyes.

"In Glenaladale they sharpen claymores," he murmured.
"On my journey to the mainland, carrying messages for
the Laird of Kinlochmoidart there was only one question
asked of me."

"And that?" asked the Duke quickly.

"When will he come?" replied Alastair.

CHAPTER VI

OF EYES THAT WATCHED

AWAY over the distant glens beyond the mainland the last
flicker of lightning died amid the storm, and the black
clouds rolled away and the dawn came up in a blaze of red
glory that tinted tree and heather.

And with the dawn . . .

Little boats upon the calming sea and a Prince come home.

Alastair had been glad of a rest after the adventures of
the night, and the sun was well over the edge of the world
when he awoke to find that already the Prince's party had
gone ashore.

Coming on deck, he found a few French sailors looking
with interested eyes towards where Erisca lay bathed in
sunshine.

They helped him to get the jolly boat away, and it was
O'Sullivan who aided him to draw his tiny craft up the

beach, for O'Sullivan, having business aboard the *Doutelle*
was returning to the ship.

"Ah, Macdonald!" he exclaimed. "We left you to a well
deserved rest."

O'Sullivan, before launching his boat, pointed out to
Alastair the direction taken by the Prince's party, and
in a humble cottage, filled with peat smoke, Alastair found
Prince Charles Edward.

The Prince was conferring with Sir John Macdonald
but the Duke of Athol, seeing the new arrival, beckoned
Alastair over to him.

"Macdonald," he said, "I want you to get to Glenaladal
with all the speed and with all the stealth you can command
for at any moment now the arrival of Prince Charles may be
made known, and we want your kinsman to be prepared."

"Take this," he added, "and let Clanranald have it as
soon as you possibly can. Give your life for it if need be
for if this gets into English hands our cause is all but lost
—remember."

Alastair took the package.

"I will guard it with my life," he said, "and at the worst
lose my life—the paper shall never get into the enemy's
hands."

Leaving the cottage, he chose a different path from the
one upon which he had beached the jolly boat, and upon the
beach, as the Duke of Athol had informed him, he found
sailing boat.

Alastair, as has been seen, was an expert with a sailing
boat in fair weather, and now it was but the work of
moment to get the craft under weigh and racing toward
the mainland with a breeze that was coming over the
island.

Alastair's journey was a long and dangerous one; but
at last he made the mainland, and found that he had struck
a rocky and uninhabited shore.

Alastair had been given money with a reason. There
was a horse to be bought at the first opportunity, and the

opportunity arrived that afternoon when, footsore and hungry, he arrived at a farm.

He had seen this spot from the top of a mountain path and had hurried down to find it was a small but well-kept place. Oaken beams and aged cement kept the walls together, and behind it the pine woods dreamed away into the distance.

Alastair's face was flushed with the exertion of hurrying over rough country. His shoes bore evidence of the roughness of the roads, and his kilt had been torn by bracken and bramble as he had hurried along.

But his bonnet, Prince Charlie's own bonnet, was gay and jaunty, and there was a song on Alastair's lips as he came through the little clump of trees that hid the farm from view on the level land, and at last saw his objective.

But Alastair saw something else.

Tethered to the last of the trees before the farm was reached were six horses, and lounging in various attitudes of ease outside the farm itself were six redcoats who, in the lowland tongue, were making merry with an aged Highlander who, so it seemed, had but recently been ministering to their needs.

For a few moments Alastair hesitated.

If he moved forward it meant danger, and he could ill afford to let his own adventurous spirit interfere with the Duke of Athol's plans.

He decided quickly. The next moment he was carefully hidden in the brushwood, watching events.

"So this is the best whisky you have, is it?" asked a brawny corporal of horse, looking towards the Highlander.

"Aye, and the last drop for ye," came the quick answer. "It's more than enough you've had already, my bonnie mon."

The corporal flushed with anger and rose to his feet.

"You'll be stopping me from having some more maybe?" he said viciously.

The Highlander did not speak. Leaning against the

door-post, he looked at the angry corporal, who now approached him with a most menacing air.

"Come back, Hawkwood," said the sergeant. "Don't be a fool, man."

But Hawkwood had been fired with a bravery he had never shown at Fontenoy.

The next moment his fist flashed out, but the Highlander avoided the blow.

Hawkwood stood for a second surprised that his stroke had been unavailing, and the pause was his undoing, for the Highlander, with the litheness of a cat, was at him and had picked him up as though he had been a child.

Raising him in his arms he bore him to a pond that stood to the right of the farm and, with a great heave he threw him, in all the glory of his scarlet tunic, into the mud and the water.

"Let that cool ye, mon," said the Highlander. "If I had been younger you would have had cause to regret that blow even more. Let it be a lesson to ye."

With that the old Scot turned and walked back to the position he had left, nor did his face show sign that anything out of the ordinary had happened.

Alastair had watched the incident with genuine amusement. Perhaps it had been better for him had he laughed a little more discreetly, for, as Hawkwood crawled out of the pond, Alastair heard a light, sarcastic laugh behind him and, springing to his feet, faced some one whose sneering eyes the lad knew only too well.

CHAPTER VII

ALASTAIR FACES A GRAVE SITUATION

FOR a moment neither of the two spoke. Alastair was looking at the smart uniform of the newcomer. The red coat and three-cornered hat. The trim sword and the spotlessly white cross-belts. The white breeches and the gold at the newcomer's breast.

Then Alastair laughed. To him it seemed so strange to see that long saturnine and gloomy face above such a riot of colour.

"They've made a mighty fine change in you, Saul," said Alastair, trying to keep back his laughter. "You look the real lobster now."

Cornet Saul Harding of the Dragoons drew himself up and looked scornfully at the gay-eyed lad facing him. He eyed the jauntily set bonnet and the white cockade that stood out against the black velvet of it. He looked with wonder at the small silver buttons on the little coat and the buckles of Alastair's shoon.

"Seemingly *you* have found service as well," he answered coldly.

"Since I was turned out on your account, dear brother, what else could I do?" asked Alastair.

"Where did you thieve that bonnet and coat from? I'll warrant me you never came by them honestly."

Alastair smiled.

"In that you speak with your customary ignorance, Saul," he answered, "for they were given me but recently by one of my own clan and they once belonged to a friend I have not long left—a good friend in whose service I now am."

Saul Harding sneered.

"It was a fine day when the Hardings married into an impoverished Scots family," he said bitingly.

"And how is my dear mother?" asked Alastair lightly. "Proud no doubt of her gallant son, and not worrying over much as to my whereabouts?"

"No," said Saul sharply. "And neither does your father, not that I have any too much respect for him," he added.

Alastair laughed.

"Did he force you into that coat then?" he asked. "And with the wars with the French in full swing it would be sad if such a gay creature stained his plumes in the whirl of battle."

Saul's hand fell to the hilt of his sword, but looking at the useful little claymore his step-brother carried, he refrained from putting the thought into action.

Alastair saw the movement, and glanced keenly at his step-brother.

"Why not obtain help, Saul?" he said. "Those men no doubt are at your command. Heaven forefend that I should stain your sword!"

Saul's face was a picture of indignation, and now he was glimpsing Alastair with the craftiness and cunning that had always exasperated the young Scot.

Saul came nearer to Alastair and the hateful sneer had developed into something like a snarl.

"We saw to it that Fiona knew," he said. "Fiona, who thought you such a hero."

Saul smoothed his uniform down and then looked at his gloves, and his eyes were full of craft.

"When I told her you had been forbidden the house, when I explained why you had gone, that you weren't to be trusted, she was sensible enough to fix her affections on some one more worthy of her."

As Alastair heard this the red blood surged through his veins. He realised now how he had been duped. No doubt it was Saul who had had his cousin Fiona sent south just

efore the quarrel that severed Alastair from his father for
ver, and Fiona had been Alastair's constant playmate and
riend, and latterly something greater than friendship had
egun to grow in two young hearts.

The next second Saul experienced the effects of a truly-
imed blow.

"You hound!" exclaimed Alastair. "Not satisfied to
oison my father's mind with your lies you have sought to
urn Fiona against me as well."

Saul Harding crawled painfully to his knees and felt his
hin to see if it was still whole. Having thoroughly satisfied
imself that it had not been broken, he snatched at the
whistle in his baldric and the next moment a silvery note
was ringing amid the trees.

Alastair smiled grimly and loosened his claymore, for
oming through the trees at full pelt were three troopers,
ed by the sergeant of horse.

They came upon a pretty sight. Standing, with his
back to a tree was a keen-faced lad with a glittering eye and
a shining and sharp claymore, whilst their officer lay
foolishly in the brushwood with a chalk-white face, made
even more ghastly by the red of his tunic.

"Arrest that scoundrel, Bold!" he said angrily, looking
at the sergeant and then indicating Alastair.

There was an amused look in Sergeant Bold's eyes. He
had no love for the young cockchafer but newly come north,
with a commission won by influence at Court.

"Don't wait, man!" cried Saul, rising to his feet. "Do
as I command."

Sergeant Bold approached Alastair.

"Come, my lad," he said. "You can't fight five of us.
Hand over that toy sword of yours."

Alastair laughed in his face.

"If your officer makes one of the five," he answered, "you
can reduce the number of my enemies to four—*he* can't
use a sword."

Sergeant Bold was a man of action as well as discretion,

and there was a certain admiration in his mind for this la
with the brave look.

"Blake, Day and Bowley," he said, turning to the thre
troopers, "get behind him while I engage frontally."

Sergeant Bold's sword flashed out and met Alastair's stee
and the play of cut and thrust began whilst Blake, Day an
Bowley, drawing their sabres, took up the fight to bot
sides and behind, with the result that before Alastair ha
made many parries and thrusts his sword had been wrenche
from his grasp by the same trick that "Red Angus" ha
used when he had disarmed Alastair at Glenaladale.

Alastair bared his fists, but Day's great arms were abou
him, and with Bowley's help the young Macdonald wa
carried back towards the farmhouse, with Saul and Sergean
Bold bringing up the rear.

The old Highlander watched their coming with eviden
interest, but he did not speak nor did he make any attemp
to interfere with the red-coats.

"We must look after this fire-eating fellow," said Saul to
the Sergeant. "If my instinct tells me anything he is a sp
against us, and I have reason to believe, Sergeant, that ther
is trouble brewing here in the north."

The Sergeant nodded with the deference due to an officer
but a strange smile hovered about the old campaigner'.
mouth, for truth to tell he would have preferred it had
Saul been something like this Scots lad, whose small clay
more the Sergeant was holding with the respect due to a
gallant foe.

"But he is a mere lad, sir," said Sergeant Bold at last
"What part could he play, and how could the Jacobite
faction make use of his services?"

Saul sniffed contemptuously.

"He has no side," he answered. "He would serve where
most money could be obtained."

"You seem well acquainted with the lad, sir," said the
sergeant.

The Cornet of Dragoons flushed,

"I have the misfortune to be his step-brother," he said. "But there, Sergeant, I am not to be blamed for the faults of my mother."

Sergeant Bold was restraining his laughter with difficulty, for it had not taken him half a moment to see that Alastair came from a stock that possessed courage as well as high breeding, and the sergeant, who had served under General Harding, one of the victims of Fontenoy, knew that Harding had risen from the ranks.

"Have Macdonald trussed up and put into a barn," said Saul authoritatively.

Sergeant Bold saluted and, entering the farmhouse living-room, gave instructions for the pinioning of Alastair, who, when the bonds had been made firm, was carried into an outlying shed and left there, with a trooper on guard.

As hour followed hour Alastair heard nothing save the relentless step of the sentry guarding his prison. At times he heard Bold's voice, as the sergeant changed the guard, and at last Alastair, tired out and sick of heart, slept.

It was a softly-whispered injunction to be silent that awakened Alastair and, looking up, he saw the light of a lantern and bending over him was the old Highlander and, wonders of wonders, a knife was severing his bonds.

"Whisht, mon!" murmured the old Scot. "The guard is as drunk as though he had been to a wake, old Graham saw to that, and yon the officer and his men are making merry with my whuskey. Here's your bonnie sword, laddie, and maybe you can give a good friend of King James a word of hope and encouragement as to the future, for I saw the cockade, laddie, and I know its meaning."

Alastair gripped the old man's hand and whispered the news of Prince Charlie's coming. Then Alastair rose stiffly to his feet and worked his arms up and down to bring the life back to them.

"We are all ready here, bonnie lad," whispered Graham. "Too ready, and it is for that reason the southron horse have cam to the glen. You'll find the others ready as you

ride, and tell the good Clanranald so. One hundred sword
from here alone, and that is every man who can wield one
and some laddies like yersel as well."

Alastair took the claymore and sheathed it, and then
with a last expression of thanks to the old Scot and a last
handshake, stole out into the night.

CHAPTER VIII

THE GATHERING OF THE CLANS

DRUMS amid the glens and the skirling of the pipes; horses
on the roads and the marching of men; riders going east,
west, north and south, with the same message to all.

"He has come!"

Alastair had done his work well. The rest of his journey
to Glenaladale had passed without incident. The Duke of
Athol's letter had been handed to Clanranald and Athol's
instructions had been carried out to the letter.

The clans were gathering. Just as the white mists gather
over the fair waters of Loch Shiel, so all bedight with
claymore and buckler came the clansmen to the call.

There had been hours of suspense. There had been
moments at Borodale on the Mainland, where Charles
Edward had landed after leaving Erisca, when the cause of
the Stuarts hung in the balance.

The Macdonalds, cautious and careful for their Prince,
had begged for time—the moment was not ripe they said;
there was a dearth of leaders—of money.

Clanranald, Glenaladale, the elder Clanranald, Kinlochmoidart had all begged for time, so that Prince Charles
Edward, glancing around at his counsellors, felt the high
colour mounting to his cheeks to betray the shame and
anger he felt at these cautious counsels.

Alastair had ridden to Borodale with Glenaladale, and

now, standing on the edge of the gathering, watching the
Prince's face, he felt a wave of indignation passing over
him.

Prince Charles saw Alastair's look and, seeing, understood,
and rising to his feet he swung towards the young Macdonald.

"Will not *you* help me?" he exclaimed.

Alastair did not hesitate.

"I will, I will!" came his ringing answer. "Though not
another Highlander should draw sword for you, I will."

Alastair's natural emotion had been infectious, and now
the clans were gathering. All the sage and dangerously
cautious advice had been swept aside, and in one moment
the Macdonalds had made their decision.

And the message had gone south as well.

In England there were strong camps of the Stuart cause,
and already many an old believer in the Stuarts was riding
north and carrying on the message as he rode, and so one
day . . .

Through the trees that concealed the road from Lochavon
House a jaded rider appeared and, dismounting from his
horse, threw the bridle over the iron staple at the house's
entrance and then knocked on the oaken door.

No answer came from the house, but from the shadows
of a tree an old man appeared. It was Kenneth and his
eyes were keen and bright.

"Sir John Daveril?" he murmured.

The horseman turned and, recognising the old man,
stretched out his hand.

"Kenneth Macdonald!" he exclaimed. "So your great
wish is granted at last—he has come!"

Kenneth smiled.

"Aye," he answered. "He's come, sure enough, and no
doubt you have come to follow him."

Sir John Daveril's eyes were alight with loyalty.

"The Stuart cause was *always* our cause," he said. "You
ever knew that, Kenneth."

Kenneth nodded his white old head, and a sad look came into his eyes.

"My kinsman will not ride with ye, Sir John," he said sadly.

Sir John gripped the old man's arm.

"He's not dead, Kenneth, don't tell me that Hamish Macdonald is dead."

"Aye, he's dead enough," was the reply, "but not dead in the flesh so much as dead to the cause that is Scotland's cause and England's cause as well."

Daveril started back.

"Hamish Macdonald no longer a Jacobite?" he said softly.

Kenneth lowered his head with shame for a moment, but the next he had raised it and was looking full in the cavalier's face.

"Puir fool!" he said. "He's had his loyalty to Prince Charles and King James knocked out of him by the woman he married, but thanks be to God his son is now with Prince Charles; for riders have been here, Sir John, but not to call Hamish to the clan. They came for *me*," said the old man proudly. "And I start to-night for Glenfinnan, and not alone . . ."

"You will ride with me, then?" said Sir John Daveril.

"Aye," came the answer. "And with another, the Macdonalds of Lochavon will make up for the lack of their Laird. There will be three of us, and the third will be a girl. Shame take my kinsman Hamish!"

Sir John Daveril turned away from the door.

"It would be better if I did not see him," he said.

"So it would," answered Kenneth. "I'll take your horse, and see it fed and watered, and I can find a place for you, and we'll set off with the morning, for Miss Fiona will be with us, ready to join Bonnie Charlie."

"Come with me now, Sir John," he said softly. "We must not be found here . . ."

CHAPTER IX

THE STANDARD

THERE were three men in the echoing hall of Glenaladale House—three men with grave faces and firm lips.

"Your Royal Highness is tired?"

It was Glenaladale himself who spoke, and, as he did so, he took Prince Charlie's riding cloak and laid it on a chair and glanced at Clanranald.

"You must sleep," said Clanranald softly. "Listen to the wise counsel of Glenaladale and spend the night here and ride to Glenfinnan to-morrow. We can send Alastair to prepare the way for your coming."

"Well, well, Clanranald," said Prince Charles, "perhaps you are right. After all, the train has been lighted, and we can but wait for the explosion. I will travel by water to Glenfinnan; we will start early."

With that Prince Charles Edward rested his head against the chair in which he was sitting and, nature asserting itself at last, his eyes closed and a few minutes later he was asleep.

Clanranald and Glenaladale exchanged glances.

The former shook his head as he gazed at the sleeping Prince and then, linking his arm in that of his kinsman, he drew Glenaladale down the room.

"I do not like the look of things," he whispered. "Sir Alexander Macdonald has refused his aid, and if to-morrow the glen be empty . . .?"

Glenaladale forced a smile.

"*Our* support is given, Clanranald," he said quietly.

Clanranald sighed and looked back to where, with his head resting back on the chair, his dusty boots spread out beside him, Prince Charles Edward slept.

"Pray God it be not a sad home-coming," he said softly.

At that moment "Red Angus" was busily engaged in a matter which gave him infinite satisfaction, and he was being helped by Alastair Macdonald.

With his velvet jacket off and his sleeves rolled up to the elbow, Alastair was carrying swords from the armoury out into the moonlit grounds of the house.

And no sound attended his work save the occasional clink of the steel.

Perhaps this fact was peculiar in view of the men mustered there. Three lines of men stood back in the shadow of the tall trees and as Alastair passed along the first line it faded into the depths beneath the trees, and so with the second line and the third line.

The men had come in silence and they departed in silence —and all of them armed.

"One left, Angus," said Alastair. "You made a mistake, there was one too many . . ."

"Red Angus" laughed.

"There was no mistake, laddie," he answered. "There could be no mistake—I know my children, and they know me, and their number tallied with the number of swords I possessed."

He had barely finished speaking when, on the path without, there came the sound of a tapping stick.

The newcomer came but slowly, but what amazed Alastair was the straightness of the course that the man kept, and the boy marvelled at the height of this figure.

It was then that Alastair saw.

The man was blind.

"There was no mistake about the number, laddie," said Angus. "Give him the last sword."

Alastair approached the blind man and placed the claymore's hilt in his outstretched hand. The fingers closed over it as though they had been pieces of bent steel and, without a word, the blind man turned and walked back into the night.

"Would to God," said Angus, "Sir John Macdonald had

seen Blind Graeme as we saw him then, Alastair, it would have shamed him into leading his clan for the Prince."

"Alastair . . ."

The cry came from the passage behind, and turning, Alastair saw his kinsman Glenaladale.

"Get to horse at once, Alastair," said Glenaladale hurriedly, "and ride with all speed to Glenfinnan to rouse the glen, for to-morrow Prince Charles Edward goes to raise the standard there—you have no time to waste, so saddle and ride at once."

Glenaladale hurried away and "Red Angus" caught at Alastair's arm.

"I'll saddle for you, laddie," he said. "Go and get your coat and sword and I'll be ready for you in no time."

Alastair ran back to the armoury where he had left his velvet coat and, slipping into this, he set the lace at his neck and at his sleeves correctly and slipped his baldric over his shoulder. Then he sheathed his claymore and slipped it into the baldric.

Setting his jaunty little bonnet on his tumbled hair, he ran back into the grounds where Angus was just finishing the saddling of a high black horse.

Glenaladale had given Alastair this mount for use in his service, and he had christened the mare "Fiona."

"Up with you, laddie, and ride like the wind," said Angus with a gay laugh.

Alastair slipped his buckled shoe into the Highlander's strong hand and leapt into the saddle, picked up the bridle, and with a turn of the wrist brought "Fiona" round and was off like the lightning.

"To-morrow!" he called back to Angus, and, as he rode off, there came back the distant answer "To-morrow!"

Alastair found the path with ease, for the moon made the night seem like day. It picked out tree, hill and stream with its light and inspired Alastair so that he rode with a song on his lips; and as *he* rode, others rode.

Old Kenneth, Sir John Daveril and Fiona Macdonald had

wasted no time, but it had been unfortunate for them that Mrs. Harding, parting from one of her friends who was posting south, had seen the three horses concealed by the little burn.

Her keen and crafty eyes had watched them depart, and she had blessed the Providence which brought a troop of horse to Lochavon but a few minutes after the three had ridden away. And if there was a warm welcome for her son, Saul, who commanded the troop, it was the warmer because in his appearance she saw a chance of executing a plan she had already schemed in her designing brain.

"Saul," she said earnestly, "things are not as they should be here. Old Kenneth has gone, Fiona has gone, and but a few minutes since I saw Sir John Daveril go with them."

Saul watched his mother intently.

"Maybe they go to Glenaladale," he said. "That reprobate Alastair has found service with his kinsman there."

Mrs. Macdonald smiled strangely.

"Saul," she whispered, "I have reason to know that there are some companies of the Royal Scots along the road by which these three must travel. Take the shortest route and get in front of them and have them held up. You would be doing a great service to me and to the cause to which I belong if you accomplish this, and I could make your action a very good excuse for instant promotion; there are friends . . ."

Saul Harding puffed out his chest and already imagined a captain's lace decorated his red coat.

"I'll go now, Mother," he answered. "I have a good mount, and I know the road; they are not so far ahead by now that I cannot pass them."

Mrs. Macdonald drew her son into a quick embrace and walked with him to the door and, as he mounted, unhitched the bridle of his horse, which she handed up to him.

"Stop them, at all costs," she whispered. "And now good-bye!"

Saul, settling his heavy frame in the saddle, rode off along a road that, if bad, was a shorter way to Glenaladale than the one the three mysterious riders had taken.

At last, breasting a hill, he saw the moon shining on the lower road, and just where the road he was on met the other way, some lights twinkled.

"Bivouac fires!" he exclaimed. "That must be Scott's post."

Saul's mount was nearly done, but the animal responded nobly to the last lap, and it was a sweating and nervous horse that pulled up dead to the cry of "Halt! Who goes there?"

"Cornet Harding to see Captain Scott," came the instant reply.

The sentry lowered his musket, and Saul sprang from his horse and handed the bridle to a soldier who came forward in the company of an officer.

Saul saluted.

"Captain Scott?" he inquired.

"Yes!" came the abrupt answer. "Who are you, and what is your mission?"

The Cornet told the officer in command of the detachment the reason for his coming, and, when he had done so, Captain Scott's face looked grave.

"There's something strange in the wind," he said. "I have had experience of it. The woods seem full of people, and on our little reconnoitre we have marched from mystery to mystery—do you know what it means?"

Saul shook his head and confessed his ignorance.

Giving just one glance at Saul, Captain Scott put a silver whistle to his lips.

From the brushwood by the junction of the roads fifty men appeared.

"Nothing can pass here," said the Captain shortly. "Come with me and watch the road."

Saul and Captain Scott moved from the shelter of the trees as the bivouac fires were stamped out.

"Horses, and coming this way!" Scott listened intently

and pointed down the road, as turning the bend in the distance, three horses came at a trot towards them.

As they rode, the riders were chatting, but their conversation was rudely disturbed the next moment by a sudden summons to halt and the appearance on the road of a closely formed body of soldiers with levelled muskets.

Sir John Daveril reined his mount in, and looked down at a sergeant who was gripping his bridle.

"What the deuce does this mean?" he asked.

Captain Scott and Saul ran to where Sir John was arguing volubly with the sergeant, who was doing his best to explain that he was only acting under instructions.

As the officer approached, Sir John swung round and glowered down at him.

"And you, sir," he cried. "Bid this man let my horse proceed immediately."

Captain Scott bowed.

"That I cannot do, sir," he answered, "until you explain to me the purport of your mission on this road."

"We ride to Glenaladale," said Fiona Macdonald. "I go to see my kinsman."

The officer laughed.

"That is just the trouble," he said suavely. "So many people ride to Glenaladale, and march to Glenaladale, and they do it so secretly that we wonder what is boding at Glenaladale."

This was too much for old Kenneth.

A rusty claymore he had treasured for years came out and swished through the air to fall upon a musket butt.

"Bid them dismount," cried the officer. "The three are under arrest."

Sir John realised that it was useless to make a fight for it. There was Fiona to be considered, and he felt sure that the soldiers meant business.

A few minutes later the three were under lock and key, with six men on guard outside.

And there, in that dark place, they discussed their sorry

plight whilst, without the ruined building, the sentries kept careful watch.

Fiona had just fallen asleep, with her fair head resting on Kenneth's shoulder, when Captain Scott entered the building and informed them that they were moving off at once.

They had gone barely a mile when, on the road in front of them there sounded the ring of horse's hoofs, and the next moment a rider appeared.

As he saw the party, the light of the moon on their muskets, and recognised that these were trained troops, he turned his horse and rode away.

The first rank of Royal Scots sent a discharge after him, but they did not bring him down. Seeing that the rider was making good his escape, Saul urged his horse forward and was soon on the heels of the horseman.

Rather more reckless than was his wont, Saul raced round a bend in the road at lightning speed and fell into the trap that had been set for him.

A pistol ball sent his steed to its knees, and the next moment Saul was facing a glittering claymore, held in the hand of a swordsman who, he knew to his cost, was more than his match.

Alastair's eyes were alight with laughter and the joy of combat as he faced his step-brother, and soon the merry play of steel upon steel rang down the silent road.

He played Saul back until Saul was almost into the ditch at the roadside.

" And who might your three prisoners be?" asked Alastair, as he deftly parried a thrust and sent Saul back a yard farther.

Saul did not speak. He could not speak. It was as much as he could do to guard himself against Alastair's furious onslaught.

The next instant Alastair was through his guard, and sent his sword flying harmlessly into the ditch. Alastair dropped his own weapon, ran at Saul, picked him up and threw him in the mud.

The sound of feet had come to the boy's ears, and he knew that the soldiers were not far away. Sheathing his claymore he leapt to his horse and galloped away back to the bridge.

Captain Scott, leading ten of his men, had run to where Saul, a picture of filth and rage, was standing in the mud.

"He got away," said Saul, "but I think I wounded him mortally. It was his horse's kick sent me flying into the mud."

Captain Scott placed his hand over his mouth to conceal the smile.

"We must hurry on," said the Captain. "Your horse is too far gone for you to come farther. Care for him whilst we move ahead—you will no doubt be wanting to get back."

Saul turned away and, leading his horse, walked wearily back down the way he had come.

Meanwhile Alastair's movements had been extraordinary. As "Fiona" flashed down the road it might have been noticed that there were movements amid the trees to either side of the road, and that when he reached the bridge, spanning a mountain stream, he leapt from his horse.

As Alastair did so, from behind him and before there closed in a number of armed and very determined-looking men, to whom he spoke in quick undertones.

"Scott's companies," whispered Alastair. "They are bound for Glenaladale. It would be fatal to let them through."

A broad Highlander, who appeared to be in command, nodded his head, and, speaking a word here, a word there, he sent various of his men speeding away into the night to both sides of the road.

Scott and his men, with their three prisoners, came marching on until at last they were within three hundred yards of the bridge. It was then that the Royal Scots saw what confronted them, and Captain Scott, deeming it prudent to retire, by a quick command had his detachments and the prisoners retreating with great rapidity.

Back through the night with Alastair and the Highlanders following fast on his heels, went Scott and his men until in a narrow pass by the side of Loch Lochy, Alastair and his comrades brought the companies to bay.

By this time other parties of clansmen had joined Alastair's companions, and the whole force placed itself under the command of Keppoch.

Keppoch had been the first Chieftain to receive Alastair's message, and therefore to Keppoch came the glory of fighting the first battle for his Prince.

Sir John Daveril and Fiona, watching the scene, felt the blood racing through their veins, and then the blood grew chill again, for a shot had been fired and a figure had thrown up his hands and fallen prone on the heather.

The sight of that stricken form seemed to madden the Macdonalds, who came grimly on towards that band of men.

Fiona, peering over the crouching forms of the soldiers, saw a boy with a bright claymore and a gay cockade in a little bonnet come up the rocky hillside to get at the soldiers.

"Surrender!" cried a great voice. "Surrender, and save bloodshed."

Scott looked to right and left of him, below and above, to see the clansmen advancing like an avenging host.

He did not pause.

"I surrender!" he shouted through the pass, his voice echoing down the narrow way.

"Then give me your sword!"

A lad in a swinging kilt and a little black velvet jacket with gay silver buttons had flashed forward and stood facing Captain Scott.

"Alastair!" cried a girl's excited and happy voice. "Alastair!"

Alastair turned, and, as the clansmen came forward from all points, and tucking Scott's sword beneath his arm, he gripped his cousin's outstretched hands.

"Fiona, by all that's wonderful!" he cried.

CHAPTER X

THE RAISING OF THE STANDARD

FIONA MACDONALD flushed a rosy red as she looked into Alastair's laughing eyes. All the seriousness had gone from them now that the fight was over.

"But why have you come north, Fiona?" he asked at last.

"To strike a blow as best I can," answered Fiona. "At first I had ungenerous thoughts of you, Alastair, but now I know that they were lying tales I heard."

"Saul Harding," murmured Alastair.

"Yes!" his cousin answered.

"He'll crawl back to Lochavon—back to his men," said Alastair with a laugh. "And I hope his mother will recognise him, for, as he crawled out of that ditch, it was more than I could do."

Fiona laughed.

"I didn't know, Alastair," she said, "how they had lied about you; now that I *do* know I beg your forgiveness."

As the two were speaking Keppoch was marshalling his clansmen.

Much valuable time had been lost in this little affray, and Keppoch had a tryst to keep, as had many another that day, and the trysting place was a glen amid the mountains.

And as those clansmen prepared to move off, upon the air there came the brave music of many a drum and the loud glory of the pipes.

"There will be no lack of claymores, Fiona!"

Alastair bent towards his cousin, and as he did so a great cry arose from Keppoch's clansmen.

"Lochiel!" they cried. "Lochiel!"

Now they could see these marching men. It was indeed Lochiel—Lochiel at the head of his clan marching for Glenfinnan.

As the two parties met their roars of cheering echoed through the narrow pass, and immediately Keppoch and Lochiel gripped hands as their clansmen beat their claymores upon their bucklers.

"It seems that the first blood of the fight is to you, gallant Keppoch," said Lochiel. "This will stir our Prince's blood."

Keppoch turned, and, catching Alastair's eye, bade the lad come to his side.

"We have to thank this laddie for it," said Keppoch. "He rode from Glenaladale to bid us be at Glenfinnan, and his keen eyes and keen ears warned us of Scott's men and their coming."

Lochiel extended his hand to Alastair, and with a flush of pride the boy gripped it.

"I march to Glenfinnan now," said Lochiel to Keppoch. "Hand over the prisoners to me—they will confirm the victory and give heart; you tarry for more parties of your clansmen?"

"Aye," answered Keppoch. "But I shall not be long behind ye."

Meanwhile a little boat with its small crew was making the passage across Loch Shiel.

In the bows, as the boat sped along, stood a tall and keen-eyed figure who looked anxiously ahead of him.

It was Bonnie Prince Charlie.

Accompanied by the loyal Glenaladale and his small retinue, Prince Charles Edward was bound for the assembling place.

And the boat sped on; and, near the spot where the little

river Finnan enters the loch, it was brought ashore; but there was no great gathering of welcome on the river bank, and all seemed silent and deserted.

The little party, pathetic in the fewness of its numbers, disembarked, and with no show of royal pomp or martial display proceeded into the glen.

The glen, save for its few natives, was empty, but there was no doubting the loyalty of these.

Coming forward they bent and kissed Prince Charlie's hand as he extended it, with a wistful smile, towards them. "God bless you!" they murmured.

Here he had come to meet his army and hear its great cry when he appeared. Here he had expected to see the raised claymores looking like a field of steel as they shimmered in the sunlight of this nineteenth day of August, seventeen hundred and forty-five; but instead . . .

The browsing bees and the lowing kine and the ripple of the Finnan running into the loch—that was all.

Glenaladale came to Prince Charles Edward's side.

"Have they failed me, Glenaladale?" asked Bonnie Prince Charlie. And, as he spoke, away on the wind there came just the faint note of something that found an echo in their hearts.

"What was that?" he exclaimed fiercely. "What was that? By God, I believe . . ."

"Listen!"

There was no mistaking the sound now. Led by Prince Charles Edward the little party moved to the centre of the glen, where there was a slight eminence.

From here they could see the marching body of men and there was no mistaking the figure at their head.

"Lochiel has not failed us!" said Prince Charles Edward, with quiet dignity, "and Lochiel is another name for Scottish loyalty."

In that little glen a few seemed many, and well that it was so.

The bonnets of those Camerons were gay with their

white cockades, and their lips gave forth glad cries that rang in harmony with the battle song of their pipes.

With raised swords they greeted their Prince, and, as they did so, as they surged about that little hill, the old Marquis of Tullibardine, who had waited through many a weary year for this, unfolded the flag of the cause, a broad banner of deep and rich red silk with a white space in the centre.

And then, trembling with the glory that was his, the venerable peer read the manifesto of the exiled King which proclaimed Prince Charles's Regency.

Now the skirl of pipes to the westward and the arrival of Keppoch and his Macdonalds, and later the MacLeods, until that glen began to put on the appearance of a large armed camp.

The hour had struck.

CHAPTER XI

THE SPY

MANY days had passed since the raising of the Standard in Glenfinnan, and now, with the Duke of Perth and Lord George Murray, together with many another rallied to his standard, Bonnie Prince Charlie had marched into Perth to the pealing of bells and the joy of the inhabitants.

Sir John Daveril, with many another Englishman loyal to the Stuart cause, had been given a commission, and he had been appointed commander of a cavalry troop formed entirely of his own countrymen.

Alastair's first duty on the army's march into Perth had been to make arrangements for Fiona.

The rush of the inhabitants of neighbouring villages and townships into Perth had made accommodation a serious problem, but Alastair had managed to find Fiona comfortable quarters with an old dame named Janet Carmichael.

Alastair and Sir John Daveril had found rooms in a hostelry, and this night they were both busy writing out orders for the next day.

Alastair's duty was to send riders out from Perth in search of forage and volunteers, and he was drawing on Sir John's gentlemen riders for this purpose.

It was an old room in which they worked. Whitewashed beams kept the ceiling up and the walls of the room bulged inward, as though doing their best to fall upon the occupants of the room.

Outside lowering upper storeys sought to reach out to the houses on the opposite side of the street.

A storm that had been threatening all day had broken late that evening and, although now the thunder sounded very distant and the lightning was more fitful in its flares, the rain still poured down in a never-ending torrent.

Suddenly Daveril paused.

"What was that?" he asked quickly.

Alastair shook his head.

"I did not hear anything," he answered.

"I'll swear I did," said the cavalryman. "It sounded like the rustle of straw."

Sir John rose from his chair and, raising one of the candles that rested on the wooden table of the room, he looked about him, throwing the light into the shadowed parts of the rambling apartment.

"Nothing there . . ."

He laid the candle back on the table and looked at Alastair, and, as he did so, from above them there came the unmistakable sound of rustling straw, and the next moment, snatching a pistol from its holster, Sir John raised it and fired ceilingwards.

Then, and without a word, he swept the candles to the floor, where one of them flickered for a moment and then went out. The others had been extinguished in falling.

"Alastair . . ."

Macdonald heard the whispered name, and came groping through the darkness towards his friend.

"What is it?" asked Alastair quickly.

"Some one above there," came the soft answer. "There is a trap-door. Up on my shoulders with you and raise the trap-door. Try and catch the sides of the trap and draw yourself up."

In a moment he was on Sir John's back and had pushed the trap-door back, and, with his dirk between his teeth he gripped at the sides of the trap and pulled himself into the loft above their room.

For some moments he waited, expecting attack, but none came. Only the silence of this dusty place and the sound of Sir John's heavy breathing below.

At last, realising that there was no human being within reasonable reach of him, Alastair whispered this information to Sir John and bade him light one of the candles.

Looking down, he saw the flint and steel light up the wick and a minute later Sir John, standing on the table, handed the light to Alastair.

"I must have been mistaken," he said with a laugh. "You would surely have been attacked had there been anything there—or any one."

Alastair took the candlestick and raised the light so that it could reveal the farthest corners of the loft, and, as he looked about him, he gasped with astonishment.

On his left-hand side there was the wall, but on the right the loft went away farther than the light carried.

"Sir John," said Alastair quickly, "there is something very peculiar here. Come up, can you? I've hit on a mystery, I think."

Daveril sprang upwards and caught at the side of the trap and, helped by Alastair, managed to get into the loft.

"See," said Alastair, holding the light high, "this loft runs above quite a number of houses, and it looks as though the loft had been continued on with an object."

The two walked down the loft to find that holes had been carefully cut in the masonry large enough for at least two people to walk abreast.

Sir John glanced at Alastair.

"It strikes me that we *have* hit upon something strange," he said. "We'll see this thing through, Alastair."

With that Sir John sat down and drew off his riding boots and bade Alastair discard his shoes.

"See," Daveril murmured, "there is the straw, and here is my bullet hole through the trap. It must have been pretty near, that shot of mine."

"Are you ready?" he added, and with that he crept forward, his pistol primed and prepared for any emergency.

As they went they looked for rays of light coming through any chink in the trap-doors of the houses over which they passed, but all was blackness, save for the fitful light of their candle.

On and on they went until at last, right in front of them, they saw a beam of light striking up from the floor and playing on the cross-beams above.

"I'll go forward," whispered Alastair.

"Yes, you are lighter and softer-footed," said Sir John. "Crawl above the light and look down."

Alastair lay face downwards on the floor and then wriggled forward inch by inch, until at last he could place his hand over the hole through which came the ray of light.

Nearer to the hole he crept, and then, bending his head he placed his eye above the ray and looked downwards.

Immediately below him, and looking more grim than she had seemed when last Alastair had seen her, was Dame Janet Carmichael.

Facing her was none other than his stepmother, Mrs. Harding, and for grimness her face nearly rivalled that of Mistress Carmichael.

There was another occupant of the room, a weazened-faced man.

This man, clad in a black, close-fitting suit, was washing his hands with invisible soap whilst he spoke, first to one woman and then to the other.

The dust and wisps of straw on his tightly-buttoned coat told their own story.

The man spoke in a cracked, uncertain voice.

"They are sending to Dundee for money, arms and horses," he croaked. "Daveril's men will ride. The young Macdonald is writing the letters."

He laughed harshly.

"I was fired at," he said, "but they thought to catch me too soon, that is if they ever knew I was there. Report says the nerves of all of them have been set on edge by Lord George Murray's domineering manner. No doubt it was nervousness made Daveril fire."

"And the boy?" asked a harsh voice. It was Mrs. Harding's.

"We'll soon settle with the boy," came the answer. "That will follow the assassination."

"Are your plans made, Rattler?"

This time Dame Carmichael asked the question.

Alastair could picture the scoundrel rubbing his hands as he spoke.

"All of them," came the answer. "I have found ten of the men sent by M. of Edinburgh, and have arranged that they shall do the work," he chuckled. "It is suggested that the Pretender be given a ball in his honour," he added. "I am going to see to it that the ball be a musket one and not a dance!"

"What about the prisoner?" asked Mrs. Harding, sharply.

"Safe and sound," came the reply, "and ready to be cross-examined."

"Then bring her here, blindfolded," came the abrupt order. "You will do the talking, Mistress Carmichael, you know all that I want her to be asked."

As Alastair listened, this last part of the conversation below him sent the blood draining from his face, for the full realisation of something of all importance had come to him.

Fiona was a prisoner in these people's hands. That seemed obvious, and what was more obvious still was that the whole thing had been most skilfully planned.

CHAPTER XII

TO RESCUE FIONA

CRAWLING back into the blackness of the loft, Alastair found Sir John Daveril and told him all that he had heard and seen.

"We've lighted upon something more than a mystery," said Sir John. "This is the work of Providence itself."

"We must act now and quickly," he added. "You stay here and watch the room whilst I go and arouse the guard and have the house surrounded. Take my pistol."

Sir John, with a parting word of counsel to Alastair, crawled away.

As for Alastair, he returned to his place of observation, and, just as he glued his eye to the hole, he saw the door opened and his cousin brought into the room by the man that the two women had called Rattler.

Fiona looked pale.

"What does this mean?" she asked. "Why am I blindfolded and kept a prisoner?"

A sharp staccato laugh came from Dame Carmichael.

"Silence girl," she said sharply. "There are many things that we want to know, and unless you tell it will be the worse for you."

"I will tell you nothing," said Fiona, with quiet dignity.

"Oh, yes, you will," came the sharp retort. "We want to know the Prince's plans and, as you have been with the Pretender since he unfurled his standard at Glenfinnan, we venture to think that you know all we wish to be informed of."

Fiona did not speak.

Rattler caught at her arm and twisted it cruelly, but still she did not speak.

The woman questioned and questioned, but still Fiona vouchsafed no answer.

At last Mistress Carmichael rose to her feet.

"Come, madam," she said, and her voice sounded harsher now and less like the voice of an old woman. "We will leave her to Rattler. He will make her speak."

The two withdrew from the room and, when they had gone, Rattler locked the door and unbound Fiona's eyes.

"Now, my pretty bird," he whispered cruelly, "tell me all you know or I will make you."

Fiona shrank back from his hateful presence.

The next moment he gripped both her arms tightly and glared into her eyes.

"Where do they march to from Perth?" he asked. "Come, speak, or I'll force the words from you."

Fiona gave a cry of terror—a cry that dispelled all Alastair's native caution and aroused the spirit in his blood instead.

With a soft movement he raised the trap-door and laid it back on the floor at his side.

Rattler, too intent on the matter in hand, was oblivious of anything save the extorting of news from his captive.

But Fiona, raising her frightened eyes, had seen; and perhaps Rattler wondered at her look of relief.

"Tell me," he hissed. "Tell me."

Alastair lowered himself from the trap-door and the next moment crashed into the room beneath, overturning the table as he did so.

Rattler gave a scream of terror and backed to the wall.

"Cry out again," said Alastair, "and I'll drill daylight through you with a pistol ball."

F.W.C.   C

"I promise not to, sir," answered Rattler. "I am an innocent man—this was but a joke."

Alastair eyed the man carefully.

"Since you are so anxious to know all about the Prince's movements," he said, "perhaps you wouldn't mind my asking you what your plans are and the plans of those who employ you."

Rattler forced a smile.

"In my pocket," he said softly. "My instructions."

Rattler's hand, trembling slightly, stole to his pocket and fumbled there, and then the hand flashed out.

There was no paper in it but a pistol, and before Alastair quite knew what had happened there came a flash, and the boy reeled forward, fell against the table and sank to the floor.

Rattler gave one glance at him and then looked at Fiona, who, pale and gasping, had fallen back against the wall.

"What have you done?" moaned Fiona. "Oh! what have you done to him?"

Rattler laughed brutally.

"He thought himself a match for me. He paid the price," he answered. "And now you must come with me."

As Rattler spoke he moved towards the door. Placing the key in it he turned the lock and then gripped Fiona's arm.

"Come!" he said sharply.

But Fiona struggled to free her arm.

Rattler would not be denied. Those arms that had seemed so nerveless were as strong as steel, and he picked her up and bore her to the door leading to the street and now Fiona was limp in his arms.

She had fainted.

Rattler laid her down on the floor and opened the door very softly, and opening it saw a light shining full on his face. He sought to get back and close the door but he was too late.

A rapier pierced him and, with just a low moan, he fell forward on to the extended sword of Sir John Daveril.

And Sir John, coming into the hall, threw the light of a flambeau on Fiona and then rushed above to find a white-faced figure lying on the floor of that upper room.

Throwing his sword down he fell to his knees by Alastair's side.

CHAPTER XIII

ALASTAIR'S STRATAGEM

SIR JOHN DAVERIL raised Alastair to a sitting position, and looked anxiously into the boy's face.

"Angus!"

Sir John looked impatiently towards the door. He had brought the gaunt Highlander with him, but Angus had found Fiona in the hall and, as Sir John's cry came to his ears, he had just managed to bring her back to consciousness.

Now he rested her, with infinite care, against the side of the wall and ran above to where Sir John was supporting Alastair.

Angus only paused a second to give vent to his surprise, the next moment there was a flask in his hand and a second later the burning liquid was being forced down Alastair's throat.

Alastair shivered, opened his eyes, and then looked about him for Rattler, but saw instead the eyes of Sir John looking into his own, and Sir John's glance was one of infinite relief.

"Fiona!" the boy exclaimed.

"Safe, my callant," said Angus quickly. "She's below . . ."

"And the man . . . ?" whispered Alastair. "The spy—what of him . . . ?"

Sir John Daveril smiled grimly and pointed to the sword he had thrown down as he bent over the wounded boy.

Alastair nodded, and then closed his eyes again.

Sir John now undid the young Macdonald's coat and laid bare a flesh wound in the shoulder which showed that the ball had gone through without breaking any bones.

Alastair was resting in a chair when, pale-faced and anxious, Fiona entered the little room.

Her delight at seeing him alive showed itself in her eyes, and in her impulsive way she ran to him and caught at his uninjured arm.

"You saved me, Alastair," she said softly. "Thank God the wound is not serious."

Fiona hid her face. She had only seen the golden glory of this rebellion before this night; now there was a dead man in the hall—one of the first victims of war, and death seemed a very real thing to her. If Alastair had . . .

Lowering her eyes she caught at Alastair's hand, and then her lips touched it.

No words she could have said would have expressed her thanks half so well.

Some few minutes later two separate parties were abroad in the midnight streets of old Perth.

With Fiona carrying Alastair's claymore, whilst Sir John Daveril and Angus supported Alastair himself, the victorious party made its way back to the wine shop.

On another road the losers of the throw hurried away from the city, as though Lochiel and his Camerons were on their heels.

In a rumbling old coach that creaked on rusted springs sat "Miss Carmichael" and Mrs. Hamish Macdonald, who had once been Mrs. Harding.

The identity of "Miss Carmichael" no longer remained a mystery, for the wig and the clothes had been laid aside in the flight, and now the hatchet-shaped face of a man, who was garbed in a neatly-fitting black stuff suit looked into the scheming eyes of the woman at his side.

"Rattler must have been caught," the man murmured,

"and we can count ourselves lucky, madam, in having made our escape."

Mrs. Harding was a prey to the after-apprehension of what she had gone through.

"A sorry start, sir," she said. "It seems that we have been bested—and by two mere children."

A couple of days saw Alastair fit and well again. His shoulder was a bit stiff, but the wound had been a slight one and his work with Sir John had gone ahead apace.

The evening of September the tenth, seventeen hundred and forty-five, found Perth in the throes of an excitement that the ancient city had not known for many a decade.

The skirl of pipes, the roll of drums, the marching and counter-marching of troop after troop of horse and company after company of foot, only added to the fever of anticipation that had come with the news that the Prince would march out on the following day.

Sir John Daveril and Alastair had a sleepless night.

There were orders to be given and orders to be counter-manded, and the streets were alive with sound.

The sun of the next day shone on a gay and gallant scene.

The prancing horses of Charlie's cavalry and the inspiring colours of the tartan plaids—the music of the pipes!

Alastair had visited Fiona early. His place was in the advance guard, and, as he had previously arranged with Fiona, she was to stay behind at Perth until victory for Bonnie Prince Charlie was an assured thing.

Fiona had demurred, but Alastair had insisted.

The girl had needed a deal of convincing, but at last Alastair had forced her consent, and now the two were saying good-bye.

"I shall come back in honour, Fiona," he whispered, "or not return."

Fiona seemed rather anxious to hurry this leave-taking and Alastair put this down to the fact that she wanted to conceal her feelings from him.

The girl did not speak as he said good-bye, she just looked

at him and then flushed and lowered her eyes, and then she had run back into the old house while he had mounted his horse and, with one glance back, had ridden off to join Glenaladale and the other gentlemen who rode with his kinsman.

And with the high sun on the claymores, to the clanging of bells and the cries of the Perth citizens, the march south began.

Perth seemed an empty place when they had gone. Thus, to many, it seemed strange that, at evening time, with the sky all rosy like a woman's blush, the clatter of a horse's hoofs sounded on the cobbled road as a rider spurred out of the city in the wake of the departed army.

Clad in black velvet, with neat riding-boots and a long and slender sword, the cavalier passed the gate and waved gaily to the watchman.

And the watchman, looking at the departing horseman, gave an exclamation of surprise as he saw the road taken by the rider.

"Not for the Prince . . ." he said to himself. "He rides another way. . . ."

He was correct, for the cavalier had not followed the path which all day long had been covered in a pall of dust, but had branched off it.

But what cared the rider? This road led south, and south was Bonnie Prince Charlie, and soon the clash of sword upon sword would tell of the fight's commencement.

So there was a song on the cavalier's lips and a fire in the rider's heart.

CHAPTER XIV

THE DUEL

COLONEL GARDINER, very dissatisfied with Mrs. Macdonald's account of Charles's forces, had bidden that good lady God-speed and had deemed it a sufficient punishment for Mrs. Harding's shortcomings to place her son in command of a tiny force that was to operate near the Ford of Frew, just a few miles north of Stirling, and the spot where, in all likelihood, Prince Charles's army would cross the river.

The Cornet of Horse had been keeping a weary watch for days, and as yet had no news to carry back to his Colonel.

They had been days of constant watching, days lacking in all save the trying work of vigilance, so the Coronet's failing spirits can well be imagined.

On this particular evening they were lower than usual. Saul Harding had been riding all day and was not a little tired.

To refresh himself, he rode into an aisle of trees off the roadside and, tethering his horse to a bough, threw himself down on the sward beneath the overhanging branches and gave himself up to gloomy contemplation.

Saul lay back and fanned his flushed and heated face with his three-cornered hat. Every sound in the forest behind him made him start and turn, and no doubt it was because his nerves were on edge and his ear eager for any unusual noise that he heard the sound of a voice away in the forest behind him.

It was very distant, but it came to Saul's ears so that he rose to his feet and loosened his sword and stole forward.

On through the trees he went until at last he came to the edge of a tiny glade and, peering past the last fringe of trees, he saw the rider.

71

The horseman looked as tired and hot as his steed, and the sight of the black bonnet with its white cockade at once convinced Saul that here was a follower of Prince Charlie.

Saul realised that he had the advantage. His sword was drawn, the rider's was in its sheath and its owner in no position to defend himself.

The Cornet determined upon instant attack, so, stepping into the glade, he stole as silently as he could towards the recumbent figure.

He had not counted with the horse. Realising the presence of a stranger the animal raised his head and neighed loudly —a warning that instantly aroused the rider who, with a startled cry, sprang to his feet.

Saul saw that there was no going back now, for the rider had recognised the uniform at once—here was an enemy!

"Have at you!" he exclaimed, and, with that, sword met sword.

Saul was the attacker, but as his steel touched that of his opponent a warning *riposte* bade him draw back and wait a better opening.

The Cornet stepped back and his antagonist played him carefully.

Had Saul been anything of a swordsman he would have seen numberless weaknesses in the defence of his antagonist, but Saul was not cast in the heroic mould, and the defects were more than balanced by his own shortcomings as a swordsman.

The sparks flashed from the contending steel, and now Saul was feeling that he had been just a little unwise in tempting Providence in this way.

This opponent seemed to make his sword live, and Saul was beginning to pant for breath. It was on his lips once to call a halt and surrender, but then he managed to get the advantage a moment after, so forgot his fear of the seconds before.

Nor did they know that they were observed.

As the two fought, the trees seemed to conspire to hide a large company from their sight.

Once, one watcher clutched at his claymore as though he meant to dash into the glade and end it with one cut, but he saw the little cavalier recover his position and drive his foe backward, ever backward.

As yet no blood had been drawn. Neither of the two had made a hit.

They staggered now as they fought, for both were tired.

They were all unconscious of those eyes. They little knew of the forded river and the swarm of men amid the trees.

Saul's blows regained strength, and he determined to end the thing as speedily as possible.

"Yield!" he cried.

The Coronet received no reply, unless it was the clash of the little sword on his own and then the thrust that caught his shoulder and drew blood.

But he fought on.

Now, seeing that he had made progress, the cavalier came at his foe, and drove him back and pinked him again, and at last, getting him with the point inside his wrist, forced his man to drop his sword.

For one second Saul stood waiting for the thrust, the next he was on his knees with his hands raised in supplication before that slender piece of steel.

"Yield!" said the cavalier fiercely. "Yield, I say!"

Saul's supplicating eyes were full on those of the fighter who had disarmed him.

"I am your prisoner," he said. "Spare me!"

As the Cornet said this, from the shelter of the surrounding trees there came a great laugh.

Saul looked about him, the cavalier swung round, and as they did so the aisles of the forest gave up their toll. A veritable army of men swarmed into the glen and looked with laughing eyes at the nervous-faced Cornet of Horse and the slender antagonist who had brought him to his knees.

One of them moved over towards Saul and looked down at him with contempt writ large on his face.

The cavalier, fearing that the Highlander might dispatch his late foe, moved to Saul's side.

"This man is mine," he said.

Then he turned towards another Highlander, one who seemed to be in authority.

"Are you with Prince Charles?" he asked quickly.

"Aye!" came the reply. "We are the advance guard and the rest follow fast on our track, having crossed the ford."

The cavalier flushed a rosy red and turned towards the aisle through which the Highlanders had come, just as a rider appeared.

And gay this newcomer appeared. His little black bonnet with its white cockade caught the cavalier's eye, and it seemed that the rider had noticed the duellist at once, for he rode into the glen and the cavalier came to his side and, sweeping off the bonnet he wore, looked up into the newcomer's face.

"Fiona!"

The rider looked down into those laughing blue eyes, but there was no amusement in his own for the moment.

"Alastair," the rider whispered. "I had to come, Alastair. Perth was so empty, and I can use a sword."

Alastair Macdonald had to laugh now.

"And Saul did not know he was fighting a girl?" he said. "How came you here, Fiona?" he asked, drawing her some little way apart from the Highlanders near to them.

In as few words as she could Fiona told Alastair how she had left Perth on the evening of the army's departure, how she had lost the road and how she had come to this forest, thinking it wiser to wait there until the army passed her.

"I managed to take a short cut," she said, "and it was here that Saul Harding found me—and fought me."

"He didn't know?" asked Alastair.

"Not at first," she answered, "but I believe he guesses now who it was robbed him of his sword."

Saul had been surrounded by a body of Highlanders a moment since, but these, more interested in the young cavalier who had out-fought his man, had left the Cornet to his own devices.

The dragoon, frightened out of his life at being in the enemy's camp, had taken advantage of their turned backs, and as, hearing a cry, Alastair and Fiona swung round, it was to see Saul fleeing through the trees pursued by a couple of Macdonalds off whom he had taken a good start.

"I hope he gets away," said Alastair. "He has had a good lesson at your hands and he might betray your sex to the others, for, if you do come with the army, you will have to come in that garb and as my friend. Let me think," said Alastair, pausing a moment. "I have it," he continued at last. "You are a young French chevalier. You do not know a word of Erse, English, or any other language save your own—I will be your interpreter."

"But, Alastair . . ."

"Don't be foolish, Fiona," he said quickly. "Your voice would give you away in a moment. I insist."

Fiona pouted rebelliously, and then her eyes told Alastair that she had consented to his proposal.

As Prince Charlie's army continued on its way with the main body on the road, and the reconnoitring forces flung out widely to either side and in cover as far as possible, "Red Angus," with a party of Macdonalds on the left wing, was drawn to the glade by the sight of the gathering there.

He had expected that Alastair was well ahead with some of Sir John Daveril's cavalry, so judge of his surprise to find the boy here—and with a figure who looked decidedly strange to the company.

Angus approached the pair.

His discreet cough caused Alastair to turn and realise the problem with which he was faced.

"Angus," he said, "we have come by accident upon M. le

Chevalier St. Vrie. He had been lost in this glade on his
way to join Prince Charles."

"Red Angus" smiled and looked keenly at Fiona, who
lowered her eyes, and then Angus gazed at Alastair.

"It will be rough work for the Chevalier," he said, "but
no doubt the Chevalier will be able to face the hardships.
I hear already that he has some prowess with the rapier."

Alastair flushed.

"It is a pity I cannot speak French," continued Angus,
"but"—and he leaned forward and whispered in Alastair's
ear—"no doubt good Erse woud be understood by your
Frenchman, laddie; but whether the Chevalier is a good
Frenchman or not, there is something inspiring about his
gallantry that will make Angus respect him and help him,
if need be."

The two Highlanders, who had given chase to Saul, had
now returned to confess to their failure. Saul had managed
to get to his horse and ride off in the direction of Perth.

Alastair assisted Fiona to her horse, and then, mounting
his own, rode through the aisles of trees until they came to
the road.

Clansmen were still marching towards Linlithgow, and
news had come through that Colonel Gardiner's scanty
force was well on the retreat towards Edinburgh.

There was but little chance of resting. Forced marches
were the order of the day, for, if Edinburgh was to be taken
at all, there was never such a good chance as now, with
Cope away on a fool's errand and Gardiner's men well on
the gallop home.

That night the army encamped on the east side of the
town of Linlithgow. Alastair was one of those privileged
to enter the town and go to the palace with Prince Charles
Edward, to whom he had been appointed an honorary
equerry.

At five the next morning the army was again on the move
in the direction of Edinburgh.

Alastair and Fiona rode side by side, and in the company

of Sir John Daveril's troop, which was forming part of a cavalry screen to anticipate and defeat any sudden attack by Gardiner's dragoons.

"There may be fighting soon, Fiona," said Alastair. "I do wish you would ride back—it would be easy for you to do so. Sir John has several riders who are carrying messages down the line."

Fiona laughed and shook her head.

"Not so early in the day," she answered. "It would be a sad thing if a Macdonald retreated before the fight, Alastair."

So Alastair had to consent.

It was at two in the afternoon that the advance guard marched into the village of Corstorphine, with the wind carrying the sound of their pipes to where Scotland's capital lay some two and a half miles to the east.

And two miles in front, at Coltbridge, Gardiner's rather rushed dragoons had come to a stop, as though at last they meant resolutely to contest the approach to Edinburgh.

Meanwhile those in Edinburgh who still held Jacobite sympathies were at work. They had occasion to smile at the desperate attempt made by the magistrates to marshal enough militia and volunteers to stem the Highland attack.

Fiona and Alastair, so near to the person of the Prince himself, heard the news as it came through.

Alastair was discussing with his cousin the chances of taking Edinburgh by storm when a summons came to Alastair that he was to repair at once to the headquarters of Lochiel—the messenger was "Red Angus."

"Your chance has come, laddie," murmured the great Highlander. "Your chance to take a city without bloodshed."

CHAPTER XV

THE NIGHT OF STRATAGEM

ALASTAIR found Lochiel in earnest conversation with Colonel O'Sullivan, Bonnie Prince Charlie's adjutant, and as young Macdonald entered Lochiel beckoned him forward.

"Your kinsman Glenaladale has spoken well of your resource in moments of urgency, Macdonald," he said, with a stern smile, "and Colonel O'Sullivan here and myself have a mind to test his opinion."

O'Sullivan smiled as Alastair flushed.

"You wish me to get into the city?" he asked quickly.

Lochiel laughed.

"The callant reads our minds, O'Sullivan," he said. And then, turning quickly to Alastair, he added: "You have guessed rightly."

"You see, Macdonald," he said, "you can go where others cannot—they might not suspect a boy, but then again they might suspect you, and if that occasion arises your chances of coming through alive are rather remote."

Alastair drew himself up.

"I should not take that into account," he said simply.

"Here we have the true spirit, O'Sullivan," said Lochiel. "We need have no fear of telling our own particular plans."

Lochiel now addressed himself to Alastair.

"Prince Charles," he began, "is tired of the trickery of the Edinburgh magistrates, who are delaying negotiations for the surrender of the city in the hope that Cope or some Divine Providence may relieve them. Their hopes are as slender as their courage, but this dallying does not suit our plan of operations."

Lochiel smiled grimly.

"To-night," he continued, "we are going to make a surprise attack on the city."

Alastair listened intently.

"There may be bloodshed," said Lochiel, "and if there is it will have been caused by the Whig gentlemen who try our patience to straining point."

Lochiel looked keenly at Alastair.

"There are many who are loyal to Prince Charles who have their homes in the city, and if we can avoid a fight we wish to do so. We send you out on an important duty, a human duty. We want you to attempt to get us into the city without a fight—you understand?"

"I understand," said Alastair. "How much start have I of your storming party?"

"An hour," came the quick response.

"I will make my preparations instantly," said Alastair, "and then set off."

Lochiel extended his hand and gripped the Macdonald's. "God-speed!" he said.

Alastair turned and hurried off into the darkness. He had listened intently to all that Lochiel had said, and no plan had been forming as the Cameron spoke, but now that he was alone with his thoughts he began to think round this urgent commission that had been given him.

He would have to doff his war-dress. That was one of the first essentials, and then he remembered . . .

Fiona . . . !

Had she by any chance the clothes for a disguise?

Alastair had no sooner thought of this matter than, as fast as his strong legs could carry him, and disregarding challenge after challenge, he ran through the camp in the direction of the cottage on its outskirts where Fiona had found shelter for the night.

As he came within view of the cottage a twinkling light in an upper room showed that its occupants had not yet retired for the night.

As Alastair approached, an upper window was opened,

to let in the air of the summer night, and he saw Fiona lean out of the window.

"Fiona!"

Alastair came into the radius of the light that streamed from the little window and looked upward at his cousin.

"Alastair!"

Fiona saw him and there was surprise in her eyes—perhaps because he had been in her thoughts but a moment since.

"Hurry down and let me in," said Alastair. "I want you to help me, Fiona."

Fiona did not pause to question, but withdrew her head, and a few moments later Alastair saw her in the doorway with the light held high above her head.

He hastened forward and, in as few words as possible, told her what was toward.

"Wait here," she whispered. "They found me a dress—their daughter's—she had gone into the city for safety. I will get it."

Meanwhile the night found many another who had not yet wooed sleep. The citizens of Edinburgh, behind their mullioned windows, looked down into streets that were full of unusual sound.

At the Nether Bow a sergeant of militia was inspecting the guard.

The sergeant had other duties. There was a report to be made to a somewhat worried officer, and at last the sergeant's men were left to their watch and a game of cards.

It was Duncan Galbraith, looking down towards the Canongate suburb, who saw a hurrying figure coming towards the Nether Bow.

Now Duncan, if just a little unskilled in the arts of war, was by no means a tyro in the arts of love; and Duncan had an eye for a pretty woman.

As he looked at that slim and hurrying figure that ever and anon paused and glanced apprehensively backward, a feeling that he would like to assist the approaching damsel came to Galbraith.

Duncan turned to two of his comrades.

"Here is a fugitive, lads," he said quickly.

"Instructions were that the gate was not to be opened," said Fergus Holme, another of the soldiers.

"But a mere girl," said Duncan, with reproof in his tones. "You can't let her remain outside when there is danger of the city being attacked by the rebels."

Another soldier was called, and now white knuckles were battering on the Bow and a soft voice was begging for admission, and there seemed to be the savour of tears in the appeal.

Duncan laughed heartily, and the three opened the gate and let a travel-stained and weary-looking girl, who hid her eyes before the soldiers, into the city.

Duncan now displayed his courtly manners at their best.

"You have come home late, lassie," he said softly, trying to peer into a pair of eyes that seemed strangely dark and nervous.

The girl was evidently too frightened to speak. Once inside the gate she sank down, and, putting her face in her hands, gave herself over to a flood of tears.

Galbraith was for taking her to her home, but the gate could not be left, so, making her comfortable by the guard-room fire, they left her.

The moments gathered themselves into minutes, the minutes came and went, and at last, through the night there came the sound of horses' hoofs.

"What's that, Fergus?" asked Duncan, on the *qui vive*, and peering into the night.

"A coach," answered Holme.

"Then it will have to stay where it is," said Holme's companion. "The coach does not pass through here although its stable is in the Canongate."

Now there came a hail to the gate of "Open! Open!" but the cry was not heeded by the soldiers.

With their muskets held ready they watched the coach, prepared for any ruse or stratagem that might be concealed by this apparently innocent vehicle.

"Put those muskets down."

It was a keen voice that now rang out through the night, and apparently it came from the young girl who had been dissolved in tears but a few minutes since.

Duncan swung round to find himself facing two dangerous-looking pistols that were pointed convincingly at his head.

"Tricked!" whispered Fergus fiercely, and his look at Duncan conveyed volumes.

"Open the gate—and quickly, or I fire!" said that cool and steady voice.

Outside the apparently harmless coach had come to a stop, and the driver was about to turn back and lodge his charge elsewhere when to his delight he saw the gate opened. He whipped up the horses and drove forward.

If any spur had been needed to make his horses go their fastest it came now, for suddenly a hideous yell broke the silence of the night.

The shadows of the street beyond the Nether Bow were alive with rushing figures. With drawn claymores and ready targe, a party of shouting, screaming Highlanders rushed towards the gate and beyond it, and at its head was Lochiel.

With secrecy and stealth they had followed the coach, never dreaming that the gate would be opened to let it pass, but the gate had been opened and now was in Highland hands.

Lochiel, seeing that his men were already making everything secure for the protection of the gate, hurried towards the girl.

"Madam," he began. "You have struck a great blow to-day for the Prince's cause . . ."

His words were greeted with a short laugh, and, dropping

the pistols as two Highlanders set themselves as guard upon the three prisoners, the girl snatched the hat from her head and a laughing, madly-happy face, was turned to Lochiel.

"The young Macdonald . . ." he exclaimed in amazement.

"You have done well, Macdonald, and the Prince shall hear of it—come now, there is much to be done."

Lochiel left a party at the gate and then led his storming detachments through the street towards the city guard-house.

Their first shout of victory had been heard. The night had carried that scream of the Highlanders through into the rooms and the dreams of the citizens, and now windows were opened and frightened faces looked down to see Lochiel's men marching with close ranks into Dunedin's streets.

Possession was taken of the guard-house. They captured it without a drop of blood being spilt.

There was no resistance offered in any part of the city, and the victors, glowing at the thought of this initial victory, comported themselves as befits conquerors, with honour, chivalry and consideration towards those they had overcome, and with the citizens, regardless of their political views, an even tone was maintained.

CHAPTER XVI

THE MORASS

EDINBURGH had fallen and, to the full glory of the pipes, to the clanging bells that told of victory, Bonnie Prince Charlie had marched around the city and then into it, and for the first time the citizens realised the force that was behind him and the spirit that had given birth to this first laugh of victory.

Hopes now ran high. Even Glenaladale, loyal but uncertain—was happier at heart, and with the capture of Scotland's capital new volunteers were rallying to the Stuart standard.

It floated out with grandeur from Dunedin's battlements, to tell of a Prince who had come again to claim his own, and over the border the news was being carried.

To some the successful entry into Edinburgh was a sign of absolute success, but there were other and wiser thinkers who realised that when the news of this first success came to southern ears—the seriousness of the position would be responded to with a determined effort to defeat the Stuart forces.

"Cope is still a threat to our army," said Alastair to Fiona. "And until he is out of the way any progress south is out of the question."

Sir John Daveril nodded.

"You are perfectly right, Alastair," he answered. "Those who think that the day is won are a danger to our cause, for over-optimism is one of the heralds of defeat."

This conversation was taking place in a little inn just nigh to Parliament Close.

Angus Macdonald, silent and austere, listened intently to what was being said.

Sir John Daveril turned with a laugh to Fiona.

"This young cousin of yours," he said, "has picked himself out for posts of danger. Since it has been proved that even storms off Erisca and sentries at Edinburgh cannot harm him he is sure to find other commissions."

Alastair flushed.

"We owe the capture of the city to him, anyway," said Fiona, "and his opportunities make me regret that I cannot be given duties such as Prince Charlie's leaders bestow upon Alastair."

The young Macdonald smiled.

"I'll wager you would do them just as well," he said,

with a smile. "I remember days at Lochavon when you were every inch as daring as I was, if not more so."

No victory could have had a better setting. The sun was glorious and a soft wind was tempering the heat. Edinburgh, yesterday fearful of approaching battle, was now jubilant with relief that her streets had not rung to the clash of steel upon target, had not been discoloured by the red blood of any of her sons.

Prince Charlie's preliminary successes were not unrelieved by a touch of humour—and his enemies had supplied it.

Cope's dragoons had not drawn rein until they had placed a safe distance between themselves and the Highlanders. Bonnie Prince Charlie's army had reached fabulous numbers, as far as they were concerned, and there seemed nothing cowardly in their flight.

They had had a breather at Leith, but the false news of the enemy's approach sent them flying to horse again. To North Berwick they rode like the wind, and later in the night a cry through the darkness so terrified these timorous fellows that they deserted the only brave man of their number—Colonel Gardiner, who awoke one fine morning to find that his command had vanished like the early mists when the sun shines on the fields.

Truly it looked as though Prince Charles was to have an undisputed march south.

But Lochiel thought otherwise—and he sent for Alastair. "Do you feel equal to a new exploit?" he asked.

Alastair smiled.

"I am at your command," he answered. "I would sooner be acting than idling."

Lochiel thought for a moment, and then he leaned forward.

"We would sooner Cope had not run away as he did," he said at last. "As long as Cope is a force to be counted with there is a danger to our arms. Now this is what I want you to do, Macdonald."

Lochiel paused, and looked intently at the boy in front of him.

"Macdonald," said Lochiel impressively, "we have reason to believe that General Cope will make a stand, and we are anxious to know where he will fight."

Lochiel tapped a letter he had just finished writing.

"I wish you to go south and find out where Cope's force is," he said quietly. "When you have done this you will report to Mr. Robert Anderson. There are full directions in this letter, and I have written particulars as to where you will find Mr. Anderson and in what manner you will solicit his services."

Lochiel handed the letter over to Alastair.

"Now," he said. "Do not wait, but get right out of Edinburgh as soon as you can. You will find that I have given instructions as to a good mount for you, and your kinsman Glenaladale has consented to your riding in my service."

With that Lochiel rose and extended his hand and the two shook in silence; nor did Lochiel speak as Alastair walked towards the door and so came to the street to find that a horse, held by one of Lochiel's men, was waiting there for him.

There was no thought in Alastair's mind to find Sir John Daveril, Fiona and Angus and tell them upon what mission he rode. He was all anxiety to get away. Lochiel's whole suggestion had savoured of urgency.

Alastair leapt into the saddle and, taking the reins of a fine roan mare, thanked the man who had held her, and rode off.

Through the gate and away rode Alastair, on a mission of greater importance than any he had ventured out upon yet.

Now it was patently obvious to Alastair that, if he wished to get through this next exploit unscathed, he would have to ride in a very different garb from the one he was wearing.

Therefore, when at evening time he rode into the quiet yard of a little inn, he determined in his mind that it would be well to change this fighting garb for something less conspicuous.

As fortune had it, Alastair discovered that the innkeeper had gone but the day before to join Prince Charles Edward's standard; also he discovered his good wife in tears.

She was young and very pretty; two facts which made Alastair sympathise all the more; and between her sobs she told him how they had only been married a few months and now her good man had gone.

It occurred to Alastair that Cope's dragoons must have ridden that way in the morning.

"Our army is large," he assured her, as he looked into two large and tender blue eyes. The landlady was very fair and slim and rather pathetic in sorrow.

"I need have no fear for my Keith," she whispered, "if a wee laddie such as yersel rides for Bonnie Prince Charlie. You are not afraid?"

Alastair laughed.

"Afraid?" he reiterated. "Of what is there to be afraid, with Cope in full retreat and the whole of Scotland ours?"

This seemed to hearten Keith's wife and she bestirred herself and waited on Alastair, finding him food and listening with intentness to his suggestion that she should provide him with other clothes.

"If possible," said Alastair, "I would like a black suit to wear, something that would not mark me as being a Highlander—that is what I want."

The woman laughed.

"I have the very thing," she answered, "and I believe that it will fit you. There was a man stayed here some weeks back, then he went to Edinburgh saying he would return in a few days, but he never came back."

The good woman showed him above and fetched the suit for him.

Alastair measured it against himself.

"If this was a man's suit he must have been a very little man," he said with a laugh.

The innkeeper's wife smiled.

"He was," she answered. "As weazened a little fellow as you could wish to meet, and he left me owing two gold pieces."

With that she departed, and left Alastair to change into the neat black suit.

The suit fitted him to perfection, and, when he had dressed, when he had set the lace at his sleeves and at his neck, and had tried the conical hat that had been left behind by this unknown benefactor, he wrapped up his own clothes and bore them below.

His coming had drawn the innkeeper's wife from her duties and, as with a raised light shining upon Alastair she saw the changed appearance of the lad, she could not forbear a hearty laugh.

She accompanied Alastair to where his horse was waiting and wished him God-speed as he rode off.

Alastair felt a deal more comfortable now. If he was captured or held up by the dragoons he had a good excuse to offer.

He could say with ease that he was a harmless traveller bound for Dunbar.

It had been late evening when he had left the inn, and now it was almost dark. There was no moon, and he found the road difficult.

Alastair did not spare his mount. He realised that more depended upon him than had ever depended before. It was a serious menace to Prince Charlie's left flank to have this Johnny Cope holding up the advance southwards.

Alastair's ride passed without incident, and it was as an ordinary gentleman that he rode into Dunbar, to find the place a prey to much excitement.

Cope's men, their great scurry forgotten, and pranked

out in their gayest uniforms, gave a touch of romance to
Dunbar on that summer evening.

Alastair had not come to pry so much as to keep in touch
with Cope's army. When they moved he meant to move
himself, and that night he felt fairly certain that Lochiel
was right, and that Cope had decided to make a stand.

A swaggering sergeant in the little inn, and to a large
gathering of the inn's best customers, told how at last
Bonnie Prince Charlie was going to be taught a real lesson.

"We've led him on," he said. "I remember how once
before a leader fell into the same trap. The cavalry ran
and he followed, and then the infantry got him and the
cavalry finished him off."

He whirled two black moustachios, and looked around
at the assembled company.

It was enough for Alastair.

Quietly he paid his score, found his horse, and rode,
just an ordinary traveller from Dunbar.

Alastair's objective now was in the direction of Seaton,
and thither he rode to find the Mr. Robert Anderson to
whom he had been directed by Lochiel.

CHAPTER XVII

THE MORASS (CONTINUED)

ROBERT ANDERSON rose from his chair as his visitor was
ushered in.

He had been expecting a visitor for days past. As Alastair
entered the room and doffed his conical hat a look of surprise
came into the older man's eyes.

He looked just a trifle suspicious. There had been one
or two riders garbed like this on the roads recently, and
Robert Anderson had suspected them of being agents of
the Whigs.

"Whence come you?" he asked quickly.

Alastair smiled.

"From Dunbar," he answered. "I have ridden hard—I bear a letter."

Anderson looked puzzled.

"You come from the Cameron of Lochiel?" he asked.

"I do," answered Alastair.

"Then, sir, you ride from a strange direction," said Anderson suspiciously.

Alastair smiled.

"I was set two tasks," he answered. "The first was to bear a letter to you, and the second to keep in touch with Cope's forces, but I deemed it wiser to find Cope first and learn what was toward."

"You have been into Dunbar?"

Alastair nodded and then, with a laugh, handed the letter to Anderson.

Robert Anderson took it and read it throughout.

"Lochiel asks much of me," he said. "How can I name the battlefield that Cope will choose? True, I know the positions round here but I do not know Cope's intention."

Alastair laughed lightly.

"It was for that reason I went to Dunbar," he said. "I fancied it wiser to know Cope's intentions. I found a very communicative sergeant. He looked very brave and spoke bravely. Cope will fight facing the village of Cockenzie. In the big cornfield with the ditch in front, Cockenzie on their front to the east of the Firth and the park wall of Preston to the west. A very formidable position."

Anderson bent over a rough map he had taken from the table.

"What is Cope's force?" he asked. "Did you learn. They are supposed to number three thousand men?"

"Two hundred less than that," said Alastair. "I rode in advance of them, just before the gates were closed to ordinary travellers."

Anderson clapped his hands.

"We must ride at once," he said. "Cope's position is a strong one, but I see a way of taking him in the reverse and Prince Charles must know of this."

But Prince Charles Edward had already been apprised of Cope's advance, although he did not know what position the General would take up.

On the morning of September the 20th Prince Charlie assembled his army at Duddington and, with the light of the sun shining on his serried ranks, the Prince put himself at the head of his men.

Soon the whole of the army was in movement. Through the silvery waters of the Esk at Fisherrow, and then along the old kirk road to Inveresk and past Punkie Cleuch to Carberry Hill.

Lord Murray, meanwhile, suspecting that Cope would try to fortify Fawside Hill, marched his men up it, only to find that Cope had disregarded this precaution and was nearer the sea.

Therefore he deployed his men from the Fawside to the post road, and the whole army advanced on Tranent in full view of General Cope's prepared position.

It was too late to attack by light and urgent councils favoured the night.

CHAPTER XVIII

THE MORASS (CONCLUDED)

No sooner had Alastair reported to Lochiel as to Cope's exact position than, to test a theory that had worried him, he stole away from the massed clansmen and, as secretly as he could command his steps, made towards Cope's defences.

Alastair's eyes were keen and young, and he had noticed the efforts of some infantrymen to drag one of Cope's cannon into position, and the behaviour of this particular cannon had been of real interest to him.

He had seen it sink.

Now, in the growing darkness, he stole forward towards Cope's defences, and as he went he became conscious of a very real thing. The ground beneath his feet was growing less firm.

Once he fancied it to be simply a matter of imagination, but as he went further forward, he realised that it was more and more difficult to proceed.

"A trap!"

He said the words involuntarily as he stepped some little way ahead, and the next moment he found himself floundering in soft mud that was drawing him under with every effort that he made to extricate himself.

He fought to lift himself but failed, and now he was down to his waist in the morass, and all hope of ever getting out of this slough had left him.

Hope dies hard though. He battled against his fear until he was up to his arms, and when the mud was making its last embrace he saw the light . . .

It flickered just some few yards away from him.

Alastair told himself now that he might as well be shot

by Cope's cannon as killed in this oozing slime, so now he shouted.

The light came nearer. In its gleam he saw a kilted figure stepping from tussock to tussock and at last the light shone down on him.

An elderly man was looking down at Alastair, and now the old fellow extended both his hands.

Alastair gripped them and the man pulled. It was slow work, but it answered, and at last Alastair stood beside his rescuer.

"You dared the morass," said the old man. "Few do, laddie. You'd better be getting home; you have had a rare fright."

"Home," said Alastair, almost fiercely. "I come from Prince Charlie's camp, and his men will attack this way. I must get to him as quickly as I can. Show me the way that I may get to him."

The old eyes looked deep into Alastair's and they were full of fear, just as Alastair's were.

"The Bonnie Laddie must not come this way," said the old man over and over again, and then he took Alastair's hand and led him back by the path towards the firm ground.

Prince Charlie's positions were in darkness, but once free of the morass, Alastair knew the direction of the Prince's position, and thither he turned his steps.

Prince Charlie was still in conference with Lochiel, when a bedraggled figure entered the Prince's temporary head-quarters.

It was Alastair.

"Thank God I am in time," he said, and then realising that he was in the Prince's presence he bowed.

"You have news, Alastair?" asked Glenaladale quickly.

Lochiel stepped forward.

"Where is Robert Anderson?" he asked.

Alastair shook his head.

"I do not know," he answered, "unless he was caught in the treacherous trap that caught me."

"What treacherous trap?" asked the Prince at once.

"The morass," said Alastair grimly. "Facing Cope's army, your Royal Highness, is something more deadly than all Cope's cannon, something that would send our army to death."

"Pits," said Lochiel.

"No," answered Alastair. "Worse than pits and plough-shares, worse than a trap of that sort; a morass that caught me in its hold and would have wrung the life out of me but for the kindly presence of providence and an old man's help."

"It was well we waited," said Prince Charles Edward grimly. "We should have marched to defeat."

"So Cope is firmly fixed, and in an almost impregnable position," said Glenaladale.

As the chief spoke the door opened, and Robert Anderson entered and bowed deeply.

Alastair presented Mr. Anderson to Prince Charles Edward and mentioned how Cope's earlier movements had been conveyed to the Prince's headquarters through the medium of Mr. Anderson.

"I cannot say how thankful I am, Mr. Anderson," said Bonnie Prince Charlie, "that we have had your services and that they have been given to the use of such a generous motive."

Anderson looked grimly at the mud on Alastair's clothes.

"I have heard rumours of immediate action," he said. "Mr. Macdonald here will tell your Royal Highness that it would be unwise to make so precipitate an attack, in face of cannon and with dangerous ground in front of you."

"Is there no way then that we can settle this matter with the early hours?" asked Prince Charles.

Robert Anderson smiled and then lifted his head.

"There is a way," he answered, "known only to a few, and a way that we can march that will take Cope by surprise, but with providence on our side we can advance in column and deploy beyond the morass."

With that Lochiel and Anderson held a conference, whilst Anderson explained the whole position, and when the two were poring over Anderson's rough map Alastair was receiving the warm congratulations of Glenaladale.

There was not a light in the Highland camp, but the watch fires of Cope's army still gleamed faintly through the mist that was rising over the morass.

Once a silvery whistle broke the silence of the night, the clash of some piled arms collapsing, the ring of steel on targe—but apart from that the night was empty of sound, although towards Cope's army an avenging host was marching, led by the intrepid Robert Anderson, who knew the secret of the morass and Cope's weakest point.

CHAPTER XIX

FACE TO FACE

THE whole army was now in movement towards Cope's well-chosen position.

Anderson knew his ground well, and like wraiths of the night the Camerons passed along that narrow passage and formed up facing Cope's cannon.

Angus and Alastair had become separated from the Macdonald clan in the darkness, and found themselves with Lochiel's Camerons.

Cope's watch-fires glimmered through the white mists of morning, for it was three o'clock when the advance had commenced; and now a great cry came from the sentries, as they rushed backward to tell of the unexpected that had happened.

How silently those Camerons had marched; but now, with the stubble of the cornfield beneath their feet, their mutterings and their cries rent the night, and they no longer marched.

A volley flashed down the line in front of Lochiel's men. With a groan a man on Alastair's right went down into the stubble, but Angus and Alastair raced on.

Now the mists were parted by the larger flash of Cope's cannon, and away on the wings there came the silvery note of a trumpet.

Gardiner's dragoons—brought to bay at last—were throwing in their weight to attempt to re-establish the scale.

The artillery guard fired furiously at those misty shapes and fired too late, for with a shriek the Cameron line was upon them, hacking and cutting, heedless of the belching cannon that cut red lanes in their serried ranks.

Alastair found himself facing a tall artilleryman, upon whose face dismay was plainly written. As the man saw Alastair rushing at him he dropped his weapon and ran.

The Camerons were on the guns now, but the artillerymen had fled.

Nothing could stay that intrepid rush. Colonel Whitney, ordered to advance by General Cope, received a discharge from so many Highland muskets that he deemed it wiser to wheel about and scatter the artillery guard, already demoralised, and when Colonel Gardiner threw his dragoons into the fray they met with as severe a reception.

Murray's regiment gave their fire and then retired, and now, with the cannon captured and the whole of Cope's line shattered, the Highlanders discarded their muskets and went into it with claymore, to make that field of corn share a double reaping.

Cope's infantrymen, mesmerised by the suddenness of the onset, had not even stained their bayonets, but had broken and fled, and only the gallant Gardiner still fought on.

"Fire on, my lads," he cried, "and fear nothing!" and crying so he died with a Lochaber axe in his brain.

There was no possibility of making a general capture in that light. There was nothing to be left to chance if the day was to be fully assured, so the fight roared towards the park walls of Preston to the west, and Cope's finely chosen position changed into a sheer death trap, for there was no getting away from those rushing, shouting clansmen, with their gleaming swords that bit to the bone.

Alastair had received a cut from a sabre, but it was slight enough to allow him to continue.

After the first blaze of fire from Whiteford's cannon, into the mist of powder smoke he had run just as the faint crackle of fire from Murray's regiment echoed above the jangle of Gardiner's squadron's harness bits and clanking sabres.

Alastair had lost Angus in the *mêlée*, for the Cameron line had become most disordered as, with victory in sight, each man wished to distinguish himself by efforts of personal heroism, and there was no necessity for organised formations now that the enemy's line had broken.

By the park wall four hundred of Cope's men had been killed and seven hundred had been captured.

Of the entire force only Cope and one hundred and seventy men made their escape.

Although Alastair's wound had not prevented him taking part in the fight by the park wall, he found it a painful enough affair when he had time to think about it.

Bonnie Prince Charlie inspected the field. He saw where the Camerons had charged, and where the MacGregors had moved across the Duke of Perth's front to join the Cameron men.

It was by the park wall that he lowered his eyes.

Gallant men lay dead here, and others were dying. Many a fading look from a Highland eye gleamed again as that little blue bonnet was doffed and as the Prince bent and whispered his thanks to those who had helped to bring him victory on that stubble field.

It was by the wall that the Prince's eye fell on Alastair.

Some little time before, and in the arms of Angus, he had collapsed from loss of blood, but now, propped up against some stones that had been broken down in the fight, he looked up at Prince Charles Edward.

"Macdonald!" exclaimed Prince Charlie, "we owe something to you this day for having been instrumental in leading our forces to victory!"

He seated himself wearily upon a stone, and looked at Alastair.

"It is plain now what Cope's plan was," he said. "He expected us to attack with the light and cross that morass. He was to have been Bruce and this our Bannockburn, but Fate and your narrow escape from death in the slime saved us from that disaster, and to-day the thanks of all Scotland are yours."

He looked at Alastair's bandaged arm.

"Mend that soon!" he said, with a laugh, "for we shall have further need of Macdonald blades and claymores before we have won our cause to honour."

Alastair flushed.

"It is only a scratch, your Royal Highness," he answered. "I would have borne more than that, and gladly, to be in such a victory!"

At that moment the clatter of horses announced the arrival of the Prince's staff. With a sigh he stood up.

"Now for a council as to the future," he said.

Alastair watched his gay bonnet until it was lost amidst a mass of cheering Camerons. Then the lad closed his eyes and, utterly tired out and deeply contented, slept.

CHAPTER XX

THE LONE DRAGOON

It was two days after the Battle of Prestonpans that a lonely figure on a rather jaded horse might have been seen riding on the road that led to the ancient city of Berwick.

The man—for man it appeared to be—lolled in his saddle, as though scarcely able to hold the reins.

His once bright Dragoon uniform was now sadly soiled, and there was blood on the blue of it, whilst the rider's helmet was dinted by a musket ball, and the tuft of horsehair had been shorn off as though by a sabre stroke.

Lonely dragoons were common sights. Gardiner's dragoons, Whitney's dragoons, Hamilton's dragoons, and sometimes a horse without a rider, following the troop, and sometimes a cavalryman on foot, who looked nervously behind him as though he could still hear those wolfish cries that had come through the morning air to rend the mists and Cope's army as well.

This particular soldier was not only weather-beaten but wounded. One arm was in a sling, and the other hand clutched at the reins as though life itself depended upon its doing so.

Once a kindly cottager bade the tired soldier halt, and insisted on giving him refreshment, and one old man took the wayfarer's horse and fed and watered it and asked about the battle with glowing old Jacobite eyes.

"You're but a lad, yourself," the old man said. "Get you home and to safety. This is men's business, not boys'."

And the young dragoon had laughed and mounted to his horse again, as though refreshed, but the turn in the road had seen the head loll forward and the body rocking in the saddle, which showed that the rider was not so tired as he appeared to be.

Just outside Berwick, and in a little clump of trees, the lone dragoon became an ordinary traveller, and the relics of battle lay buried beneath a tree stump, whilst a dapperly clad young gentleman remounted and rode away from the scene.

It was Alastair.

The lone dragoon rode on a lone commission, and his objective was to find out how strong the Jacobite feeling was, to kill, if proof could do it, the inaction that might set in at Edinburgh unless a move were made against the enemy.

Nor had he ridden without taking Sir John Daveril's advice.

Sir John's friends in England were powerful. He knew that there were Jacobite factions in London ready and eager to welcome a second Stuart Restoration; but Sir John did not know how strong the feeling was getting, or what the effect of Cope's dramatic defeat might have on subsequent events.

It was late in the forenoon when Alastair rode into Berwick.

Sir John Daveril had given the lad an address to call at, and had assured Alastair that the friend who lived there was a loyal enough Jacobite.

To Alastair's chagrin he found the house empty. He rode into the little courtyard and pulled the bell chain, but no answer came to his summons.

Sir John had been so insistent about Alastair's coming here that the boy did not want to leave Berwick without meeting this gentleman whose name was Lygoe.

It seemed very peculiar to Alastair that there was no one in charge of such a commodious place.

Tying his bridle to an iron staple at the side of the low

doorway, he turned his attention to the rear part of the house.

Here was a low outhouse, joined to the main building by a stone passage that had obviously been built to allow the occupants of the house to get stores from the outhouse without suffering the snow, rain or wind of inclement winter weather.

The passage was low, and there were no windows in it, but what interested Alastair most was that by leaping to the top of this nine-foot high building he could get above to the first storey of the house and in at a window that was open.

Alastair decided to enter the house. His intention was to leave a message for Mr. John Lygoe, and this would be safer procedure than giving it into the care of any Berwick citizen.

With the help of a chopping block, Alastair managed to get on to the roof of the building and along it, and then through the window.

He found himself now on the landing of a fine, old, oak staircase.

The staircase ran down into a very large and square hall on the panelled sides of which there were clusters of ancient weapons.

Alastair, looking upwards, noticed that the oaken stairs led to a broad gallery that ran on the four sides of the square, and that rooms led off this gallery.

The place seemed strangely silent.

The boy walked above and looked into the rooms, to find most of them neat and appearing as though they had been used quite recently.

Why he felt it he did not know, but Alastair experienced a sensation that everything was not right in this house.

It seemed gloomy now. Evening was approaching and the last faint rays of the dying sun were shining through the windows into the hall and casting long shadows that seemed to take human shapes.

Alastair walked to the nearest door and opened it. A gust of chill air met him—and darkness.

The shutters were closed against the windows.

Lying on the floor, just by the big open hearth, where logs had been laid ready, was the body of a man.

Alastair stopped, as though transfixed by the sight, and his heart seemed to stop also for a second.

The momentary pause passed, Alastair stepped across the room and bent over the prone figure.

There had been no doubt in the boy's heart that the man was dead, and this was confirmed as he looked into that cold white face.

And then he saw the cord . . .

Tightly wound about the man's throat was a silken cord. It was of the kind used to keep curtains in a neat fold, and, looking above him, Alastair saw a broken end of another piece hanging from a beam in the ceiling.

This man had died by the hand of another—or others. What did it mean?

Alastair felt suddenly afraid.

Bending over the prone figure he put his hand into one of the pockets of the velvet coat, with its bright silver buttons, and took out some papers.

There were letters addressed to "John Lygoe, Esquire," and this convinced Alastair that he had found Sir John Daveril's friend too late.

Then Alastair noticed that a piece of cotton was attached to one of the coat buttons, and now, as his eyes grew more accustomed to this scene of gloom, he saw a white paper in the clenched fingers of the gentleman's right hand.

It was a difficult matter to open that hand, but at last Alastair managed to loosen the grip and get the crumpled paper from the clutch.

He spread the paper out and read the few words written in an unclerkly hand upon the parchment.

"So perish those who follow the Stuart."

Alastair folded the paper and placed it in his coat pocket; then he raised himself from his kneeling posture.

For a few moments he looked at the dead man. Bending his head, he muttered a prayer for Sir John's friend, and then he walked back into the hall, and in Alastair's heart there was a keen feeling that he would like to avenge this crime.

As he came to the hall he found it darker, and he saw something that added to his amazement. The shadow of a man's figure had passed the window by the door that let upon the courtyard.

Alastair's brain worked quickly. It was patent to him that to be found in this house was tantamount to being an ally of the late owner.

He would go back the way he had come and perhaps, with good fortune, might manage to retrieve his horse and leave Berwick that night, for there would be no staying here now.

With light and speedy steps he ran up the staircase and came to the window by which he had won access to the house.

Alastair glanced out and the colour drained from his face.

There were three dragoons in the courtyard. They were standing by their horses and looking with keen eyes at the house.

From the front now there came a cry and the grating of a rusted key in the lock of the door.

Alastair was about to dart below and shoot the bolts, or see if they were already fixed in their sockets, when the evening light flooded the hall. The door had been opened. A soldier stood on the threshold.

The boy set his teeth and watched the silent figure.

Suddenly an unmistakable voice fell on Alastair's ears.

"Dawson—bring a rope!"

Alastair clutched at the balustrade. There would be no mercy here. The speaker was his stepbrother Saul.

With a clank of spurs the Cornet of Dragoons had come into the hall, and now he was followed by two troopers whose height and breadth almost dwarfed their officer.

"There's another of the dogs here," said Saul.

The man holding the rope laughed brutally.

"There was only one horse, sir," he said. "One man . . ."

"One rope," said Saul.

Alastair had not set out on his journey unarmed. A neat little rapier and a pistol were now his sole friends, and both these were ready as, in the gathering darkness, he stood at the head of the stairs.

"Perhaps he is armed . . .?"

Dawson's comrade spoke with all the courage of Gardiner's scurvy company. They had left him to die alone, with an axe in his skull, thought Alastair. This was work more to their liking. Something in the darkness with the odds ten-to-one in their favour.

He knew there was no means of escape. The front and the back of the house were guarded, and guarded well, by, perhaps, a troop. He would have to fight—fight to kill and then die—as others had died before him—fighting.

But the position was his.

The soldiers could only come one way and that by means of the stairs. The stairs were broad, it was true, but not so broad that three swords could engage him at once, and a ball carried farther than a thrust.

"A lantern, and sharp, Greber," said Harding. "Tell the men at the back to be on the *qui vive*."

"Aye, sir," said Greber, and ran off. Alastair heard the heavy sound of his boots on the cobbled yard without.

And the minutes dragged on.

Once or twice Saul made some amusing remark about rats in traps; and once Alastair had a mind to dare the stairs and fight his way through, but he deemed that poor strategy, with the yard encumbered by horses and perhaps more troopers ready for his presence.

At last Greber reappeared.

Saul took the lantern and, raising it above his head, threw the light upon the stairs.

"Dawson and Greber, you mount, when I have examined the rooms here," said Harding the valiant.

Next there came the sound of opening doors, a few curses and a sound of a falling chair as Saul knocked it over, perhaps nervous lest their quarry had concealed himself beneath a table.

"Nothing here."

"The light, sir," said Greber.

"Here you are," came the reply. "Now, both of you!"

Warily, and, as far as Alastair could fancy, nervously, the two troopers set foot on the stairs and, with drawn sabres, slowly mounted.

It seemed, as the light revealed them to Alastair, that Greber was not at all anxious to be ahead of Dawson, or *vice versa*, but at last Greber was near enough for a neat and clean shot at his shoulder.

Alastair raised his pistol and, taking careful aim, gave Greber the wound he should have received in battle.

With a sickly cry the man clutched at his shoulder, fell against the panelling, sank then to his knees, and then rolled like a sack of corn to where Saul stood at the bottom of the stairs.

Dawson darted back, with a cry of fear.

"Up, man," cried Saul. "You Gresh, up with you, Dawson."

Dawson, plucking up his courage and fancying that the assailant had no time to reload, darted back; and his assumption as to the pistol was correct, but the clean steel found his sword arm and sent him shrieking back down the stairs with a neat hole in his arm.

Alastair smiled grimly.

Saul cursed his men for cowards, and then called for more lights, and cried to a man without to apprise General Cope of what was happening.

Then ensued a long wait.

Saul relieved the monotony of inaction by keeping near the door and encouraging the others without to keep watch.

Had Alastair been one of a party in a besieged fortress he could not have been subjected to so much respect.

Although his life was held in the balance by the dictates of fate, he could not help smiling at these gallant gentlemen who fought so ingloriously.

But now the light below broadened. He heard the sound of cries through the night and the rush of many feet in the courtyard without, and he knew that Saul's reinforcements had arrived.

Peering below, he could see a mob of citizens and the coloury dash of uniforms, and he saw a much-brocaded gentleman forcing his way through the crowd.

He watched Saul salute and then prepared for action.

"Take three men and storm those stairs, Harding," said General Cope bitingly. "One man against all of you—pull him down."

CHAPTER XXI

SIR JOHN'S GENTLEMEN

SAUL'S sabre had flashed out, a mere pretence at courage, Gresh had come to the foot of the stairs and another trooper with him, and behind these two stood three more troopers.

Harding came forward. He had been instructed to lead his men, and there was no getting away from the command. First, the Cornet of Dragoons peered into the blackness. Alastair saw Saul's thin lips trembling as the light shone on them.

A bullet would have tightened them for ever, but somehow Alastair could not fire.

Saul looked thus for one moment, and then with a cry of

"Come on, men!" he leapt rather than mounted up the stairs.

Gresh and five other troopers were behind him and poor Gresh got the bullet intended for Saul. He fell upon the dragoon behind him and they went hurtling down the stairs, but Saul and the other four were now attacking Alastair's defence.

Alastair stood like a stag at bay. In front of him were five determined men. They had a sorry defeat to reverse, and it had to be done beneath the eyes of their commander-in-chief who had not been of good temper of late.

But Alastair's back was to the wall. He had the advantage of the darkness and his sword was like a flame of light as it darted here and there.

One of the troopers raised his sabre and cut at Alastair's shoulder, but Alastair darted higher up the stairs to his left and the wolves followed him.

It was a fatal error.

He had left the other entrance to the gallery undefended. Five more troopers lumbered above and stole up the other stairs and so came behind the lad.

Alastair had sent two troopers screaming back. Saul and two others faced him, and there were five more creeping round to take him in the rear.

He forced the fight forward and drove Saul and the two troopers before him. Saul's sword arm was pierced and his sabre dropped uselessly to the ground. One of his troopers had been pinked in the face.

The other, with the determination of sheer desperation, cut at Alastair's shoulder and won the stroke. Alastair's rapier tinkled to the stairs and he fell back against the wall as those who had come round the gallery fell upon him, their sabres raised.

One of them carried a torch, and this he shone on the white face of the lad who had fought against such odds.

Alastair had not fainted. He was leaning against the

wall clutching at his wound and they looked with dismay at him.

"A mere lad . . ."

It was a great sergeant of dragoons—the bearer of the torch—who spoke, and there was real respect in his tones as he bade his men put up their sabres.

"Honour to the defeated, lads," he murmured, with a quick glance at the Cornet of Dragoons.

Some of these men had no love for those who had so badly led them in the moment of battle.

One of the troopers picked up Alastair's rapier, and now Saul, his wrist paining him so that he winced and clutched at it at times, came forward into the radius of the light and saw it shining on Alastair's face.

He gave a quick gasp of astonishment, and the pleasure of this capture drove the pain away for the moment.

"Macdonald!"

Alastair raised his head and looked with contempt at the Cornet.

"Aye, it's I, Saul," he said defiantly. "Kill me now. You would find it easier."

Saul's face was hot with anger. There was a pistol in his belt and he snatched at it, but he never fired it, for the sergeant was before him.

"The General will want to interrogate the lad, sir," he said sharply, almost brusquely. "Hold your fire."

Then, taking no further notice of the Cornet, he led Alastair gently down the stairs, and it was to be noticed that he treated the wounded lad with all the care due to one who had put up a brave and a determined fight.

General Cope was below.

Furious anger showed in his face and his eyes. He was livid and vermilion by turns, and it seemed that his stock was all but choking him.

"Who was the man?" he shouted. "He shall swing for this night's work—bring him down."

So Alastair came below into the light of a ring of torches

that threw those red uniforms into gay relief and shone on the wounded Dawson, Gresh, Greber, and the crimson bandage about Saul Harding's wrist.

Gresh was lying stretched out with his back to the wall, and Greber was hugging his wound near to him. The hall looked like a shambles.

Cope seemed bereft of words. He eyed Alastair and then looked askance at the wounded in the hall.

"Well, sir?" he cried at last. "What explanation have you to offer for this set of murderous acts?"

Alastair, in pain as he was, wounded as he was and faint with loss of blood, yet had to laugh.

"The murderous act occurred before I came to the house," he said coldly. "I rode to see a friend and instead I found a dead man, a man who had been foully done to death."

Cope coughed and looked about him.

"What does the lad mean, Harding?" he asked quickly. "What dead man lies here?"

Saul did not speak. He lifted the torch that one of the troopers was carrying and showed General Cope the prone figure of the man Alastair had found.

"A Jacobite?"

Cope almost spat out the words.

"Yes, sir," answered Saul, having found his tongue at last. "This was not an act of any soldier, of that I am sure, sir, but after we found the body we watched the house for some of John Lygoe's friends."

"And you came upon this lad . . ." said Cope.

"Yes, sir," answered Saul.

Cope closed the door of the large room as though the sight horrified him.

"Take the prisoner away," he said sternly, "and bring him up before me at ten to-morrow morning. Guard him well, for I see that we have made a valuable capture."

General Cope then looked at Saul.

"Collect your men," he ordered, "and see that their wounds are tended to."

With that he turned on his heel and left the ill-fated house.

The clank of his riding boots on the cobbled courtyard came but dimly to Alastair's ears, for everything seemed distant now, the fight must have been a dream . . .

The next moment he had fallen forward in the arms of the Sergeant of Dragoons. Alastair had made a gallant fight against the faintness, but he had gone through too much already, and his wound was a deep one.

Saul Harding was for placing Alastair in the charge of a corporal of his troop, but the sergeant would not have it so. He made it perfectly plain to the officious Cornet that General Cope had left the lad in his care. This was done with due regard to Saul's authority, and with all the tact of an old soldier accustomed to dealing with newly-fledged cock-chafers of Harding's calibre.

So Saul collected his wounded "heroes," and the sergeant picked Alastair up as though he had been a baby and bore him off to the prison—an empty room in the billet where the sergeant was staying.

And there Sergeant Cathcart saw to his prisoner's wounds. He bathed the scratched hand and the deep sabre cut in the shoulder, and had he been a woman he could not have dealt more tenderly with Alastair.

There was some burning stuff that the sergeant had handy both for medicinal purposes and for a parched throat, and with this liquid he soon brought the light back into the boy's eyes and the colour to his cheeks.

"Thanks!" said Alastair, when at last he was able to speak. "But I am afraid you are only preserving me for a worse fate."

The sergeant laughed.

"How came ye on such a fool's errand?" he asked, seating himself on the floor, and looking at the weary lad who lay in the bundled straw in the corner of the room.

"Who knows, Sergeant . . . ?" he answered. "Perhaps bright eyes . . ."

Sergeant Cathcart twirled his big moustache and shook his head.

"I have met some rare sparks," he said, "but none rarer than you, my lad. We had done better at Cockenzie with a score of your mettle."

Alastair laughed.

"It was a sad sight, Sergeant," he murmured, and then he remembered himself; he was betraying his presence on that field.

"You were there?"

The sergeant looked closely at his prisoner.

"It was a sad sight on the stairs, Sergeant," added Alastair quickly. "The odds might have been bigger."

A smile flickered in the old soldier's eyes, and then his look was grave.

"General Cope will deal hardly with you in the morning, laddie," he said grimly. "Things have gone against him, and he suspects spies all around him."

The sergeant looked at the door to see that it was carefully closed, and then he leant forward.

"Only to-day," he added, "a rider came in from Cockenzie way and brought disquieting news of the approach of the Stuart forces. Cope is worried out of his wits."

The sergeant paused a moment.

"Mighty fine company I found that rider," he said, with a hearty laugh. "As loyal to our side as any I have seen, and I took the fellow's word. He's coming to see me to-night, in case we are off soon, for he has friends south and wants to warn them in time."

The sergeant winked.

"And he's bringing a bottle of something good," he added with a smile. "An uncommonly fine fellow this new friend of mine."

With that the sergeant withdrew, and left Alastair to his own devices.

There was no hope of escape. The lad saw that at once,

for the windows of this place were barred and he was on a high storey.

The sergeant's friend seemed a long time coming. Many minutes passed, and then in the distance Alastair heard a clock striking the hour.

The sergeant's companion had evidently forgotten his promise, thought Alastair, as, with a feeling of painful tiredness, he sank down to the straw and prepared to give himself up to sleep.

Macdonald had barely closed his eyes when there came the sound of footfalls on the stairs without, and the sound was followed by a laugh and then the grating of a rusty key in an old lock.

The door was flung open as Alastair turned to blink into the light of a torch held above Sergeant Cathcart's head.

"Here's the lad I spoke of," said the sergeant. "The rarest little cockchafer you could meet in a month of Sundays. Held the stairs against a squadron, that he did."

As Alastair's eyes grew accustomed to the light he could see a slim-figured individual standing just behind the sergeant.

A three-cornered hat shaded the newcomer's eyes and a high stock almost covered his chin, so that only a little of the face was discernible.

Alastair bowed to the newcomer, who responded with outstretched hand which, to Alastair's surprise, seemed strangely soft and slight for that of a gentleman rider.

Sergeant Cathcart looked at Home and smiled.

"A game lad," he said. "What say you, Mr. Home?"

Home nodded and then, in a low voice, complimented Alastair upon the fight. "Although," he said, "your views and mine, young man, are of a different nature, I always did and always shall respect a brave man and a gentleman."

"And I agree, sir," said the sergeant, already somewhat in his cups, as Alastair was quick to observe.

"Hold the torch, sir, whilst I go below," said the sergeant

to Home. "I promised the lad a sup of something helpful before he meets General Cope, and I'll keep my word. I've left the bottle below."

Home took the torch, and Cathcart lumbered away and below to where he had left the precious liquor.

No sooner had the sound of his footsteps died away than Home came close to Alastair.

"Have patience and courage, Macdonald," he whispered. "I ride for Sir John Daveril. I am one of his newly joined gentlemen, and followed fast on your track, as news had come of Mr. Lygoe's death. Pretend to join Cathcart in his carouse, but let Cathcart do the drinking, for he is nigh gone now, and soon a clear way for escape will be open to us."

Alastair, too amazed to speak, felt his heart beat fast, but when Cathcart returned he took pains to conceal his relief and his face was gloomier than ever the sergeant had seen it.

So much so that Cathcart insisted on Alastair drinking first, which Alastair did, and he blessed the darkness for concealing the wry expression that crossed his face as the fiery spirit passed his lips.

With Alastair's fate almost certain, and sure in his own mind as to the trustworthiness of his visitor, the sergeant began to chat about what had passed and what Cope's future movements were.

"Cumberland will be in this now," he said, banging the glass down on the floor at his side. "Cumberland will get them like rats in a trap when they come south, you mark my words, Mr. Home."

From discussing prevailing affairs Cathcart launched forth into stories of his experiences fighting the French on the Continent and each battle needed punctuating with a longer drink than the one taken before it; so that by the time Cathcart had described the French victory at Fontenoy he was well on the way to complete slumber.

He lay back on the straw, and at times roused himself to

continue the tale of his many adventures, but at last he gave it up and succumbed to the effects of Mr. Home's hospitality.

Home and Alastair sat watching the incapable gaoler, and only when it was evident that nothing short of the crack of doom would wake him did they exchange a word.

"Shall we bind him?"

Alastair bent forward and whispered the words to Home, who shook his head.

"There is no need," he answered. "Cathcart had a companion, but the sergeant was so sure of himself that he gave the fellow leave."

Home smiled into Alastair's eyes, and Alastair fancied that there was something dimly familiar about that smile.

"Behind the house you will find my horse," he said quickly. "I want you to take that and ride back to Sir John's headquarters."

"But *you*. What of *you*?" asked Alastair.

Home laughed lightly.

"I can easily find another," he answered. "Your case is most urgent."

"Take this pistol and this sword," he added, "and make yourself look as spick and span as you can under the circumstances."

Alastair did not wait.

With Home's assistance he put his clothes to rights and rid himself of his arm sling.

Next he took the sword and the pistol and hurried below, after he had given Home a hearty handshake.

Alastair found the horse as Home had directed, untethered the grey, and, mounting to the saddle, rode into the streets of Berwick.

But then a sudden despair fell upon him. He had forgotten the most important thing of all. The gates would be closed.

He had a mind to leave the horse and try the walls, but

on second thoughts he determined to do his best to get past the guardians of the gate that led to the Cockenzie road.

Towards the gate Alastair rode, and, nearing it, he drew his mount into the shadow and watched the portal.

On the right he could see the light that came from the little guard-house. He heard the chink of coins, the sound of a coarse laugh—a curse and then the rattle of a dice box.

Once the light was obscured, as a figure came into the doorway and looked into the night, but, seeing nothing, went back to the wine and the game.

Alastair waited there. Like a silent sentinel he sat his horse and watched the gate. One or two desperate ideas connected with holding up the guard had come to him, but he had dismissed them as being foolhardy.

Suddenly, from beyond the gate, there came the sound of cries.

"Open! Open! Open, for pity's sake, open!" was the plea that issued evidently from a pair of parched and tired riders.

The game ceased abruptly. The sentries ran out. One watched the road, and what he saw satisfied him that the gate should be opened.

Alastair gripped his reins tightly and watched the gate roll inwards, and saw, just outside it, two soldiers on one jaded horse.

One of the soldiers was seated behind his comrade, who, it was evident, was badly wounded.

"They caught us, but we managed to get away . . ."

Alastair heard the words and decided at once. With a cry to his horse he rode hard at the gate.

Had he been a ghost or a wraith of the night he could not have given those sentries more surprise than he did. They turned to see a grey horse come tearing towards them.

Even the jaded animal that was preparing to enter the gate sensed the sound of the approaching hoofs and it began to plunge.

Alastair had hardly enough room to pass, but he did not care for that. He rode one sentry down and cut at another who sought to obstruct his passage, and like a flash he was through the opening and out into the country, with a laugh on his lips and five musket balls rattling behind him.

The sentries loaded and fired again, but this time it was at another figure that, following the lead of Alastair, had ridden hard through the gate.

And both figures rode on, with Alastair well ahead. The rider who had followed seemed to have suddenly grown unsteady in the saddle, although two delicate hands clutched at the reins and sought to steady the rider.

Alastair, coming to a bend in the road and hearing the sound of hoof beats on the road behind him, turned.

He watched the distant horse coming along at a fairly good pace, and with a grim smile the Macdonald drew his pistol and saw that it was ready primed.

Then he drew back into the shadow of the trees and waited.

After what seemed to be a long time the pursuing animal came abreast of Alastair and, when it did, the Macdonald's expression changed.

There, swaying to and fro in the saddle, holding on with a last effort, was Mr. Home and none other.

Macdonald drew his horse in and did his best to lift Home to the ground. It was a difficult job, but he managed it at last, and finally found himself with Home lying on the grass by the wayside and the two horses safely tethered in the shadows beneath the trees.

"Home!" he said. "Are you badly hit, Home?"

But no reply came. The eyes of his friend were closed.

With nervous hands Alastair bandaged Home's wound and then, with intent to bring his friend back to consciousness, he set off in search of water.

The musical ripple of the not far distant burn drew him towards the stream, from which Alastair filled his hat.

Then he ran back and dashed some of the water over Home's face, and, taking off the gentleman's hat, prepared to bathe the sufferer's forehead.

But as Alastair raised the hat, and looked anew into the face of the wounded Home, he started back with an exclamation of surprise.

No longer did the hat and the choker conceal the face. There was no mistaking it now, although the hair was cut short.

"Fiona!"

With a gasp of astonishment Alastair bent over the still white form.

She had deceived him as well as she had deceived the sergeant, and now she lay, like some drooping lily, with her eyes closed as though in death and her poor little hands clenched, as the agony had prompted them before she had fainted away.

Alastair soon got over his surprise. There was a real necessity for him to do so. Now, he was dreadfully frightened. What if the wound were mortal? But no? This was no fatal hit, for a mere glance at the shoulder told him that the wound was but a scratch, and he breathed again as he came to this conclusion.

Fatigue and shock accounted for the swoon.

Alastair ran back to the burn and dashed some more water over Fiona's face, and then he bent tenderly over her and bathed her forehead.

But she did not open her eyes.

Again he ran to the burn, and this time, as he bent over to fill his hat with water, he became conscious of the fact that he was not alone by this tiny stream.

From near at hand there came the sound of feet as they stepped upon dry twigs, and Alastair's keen sense soon convinced him that the woods about him were full of men.

So, after all, Fiona's stratagem had been robbed of its reward by one lucky shot from a sentry.

No doubt Cope had been apprised of the ruse, and had sent out a party to find and bring the two back.

The colour left Alastair's face.

He set his teeth and, drawing his sword, crept back the

way he had come, careful not to drop the water from his hat, and praying as he went that Fiona had not been discovered.

The journey was short, but necessity made it longer for Alastair, as he was forced to hug the shadows and pause when he heard the sound of footfalls, or caught sight of a figure flitting in front of him like some strange spirit of the woods.

A gust of wind, herald of approaching storm, burst suddenly upon the trees and went with a strange laugh through the woods—a taunting, haunting laugh.

Nor did it lack meaning, for as Alastair came to where he had left Fiona lying, he dropped his hat and caught at a tree for support.

Fiona was no longer there, nor was there any sign of her by the road or near the horses which still stood where Alastair had tethered them.

And again the wind came laughing scornfully through the trees, and Alastair no longer cared for those who hovered like phantoms in the wood.

Cupping his hands, he shouted into the darkness on all sides of him:

"Fiona! Fiona! Fiona!"

Only the echo came back to Alastair.

What an end to his adventure! Fiona a captive, and all that was left to him was to return and tell a sorry tale of how, at the last, he had failed her.

The thought maddened him, and again he cried to the clouded heavens, and the echo returned with the mutter of distant thunder, and he felt a large spot of rain on his face; then the white flash of the lightning lit up the trees so that they stood out boldly against the pitch black of that angry sky.

Suddenly a shrill cry came to the boy's ears—another and another, and now he was conscious of figures emerging from the trees, and in the flash of the lightning he saw a sword gleam.

In an instant he was ready, and as a figure dashed towards him, sword upraised, he met the contending steel and the shock of the joined engagement.

"Yield!" cried a stern voice, "or it's a dead man ye'll be."

Alastair was convinced that he was going mad now, for the voice that bellowed through the night belonged to only one throat.

"'Red Angus'!" cried Alastair, above the sound of the thunder. "It is Alastair Macdonald!"

With a gasp of astonishment Angus threw down his claymore, and the next instant Alastair found his arms pinioned at his sides, and the lightning showed "Red's" eyes full on him.

"Aye, that it is," said Angus Macdonald with relief. "I fancied you were one of Johnny Cope's men for the moment."

The gaunt Highlander released his kinsman's arms, as, with frantic inquiry in his tones, Alastair asked if Angus knew ought of Fiona.

The man laughed.

"Safe and sound," he replied, "and on her way back now —it was a risky adventure for her, so we followed, in case of danger, and, finding her wounded and alone, we fancied that some of Cope's men were about. I should have struck you down had you not cried out to me."

"Thank God!" exclaimed Alastair with fervour, and then, "You ventured near enough to Berwick!"

"Aye," answered Angus grimly. "And had Miss Macdonald not returned by dawn a handful of Macdonalds would have made some history for themselves by getting at the remnants of Cope's army."

"And now . . .?" asked Alastair.

"We must get back," said Angus. "It would have been a desperate enterprise and perhaps we are lucky to escape it."

Angus had brought the horses now, and, mounting to the saddle of Fiona's steed, he led the way out through the woods to the road, and so, with heaven's artillery crashing above them, and with Fiona borne by four lusty Macdonalds, the little party began its march homewards, and soon Berwick was left far behind.

And as Alastair rode there was one thought uppermost in his mind and that was the debt he owed his cousin for having risked her life in order to save his own.

CHAPTER XXII

HAMISH MACDONALD LEARNS THE TRUTH

MANY things had happened since Alastair had left Lochavon to march to adventure in the north, and since his departure, Hamish Macdonald, Alastair's father, had learned many things.

One of these was that it was unwise to put all your trust in kings and princes.

He had learned of Bonnie Prince Charlie's landing, and had scoffed at the idea of any success attending the Prince's return, but when Cope's cavalry—or rather mounted infantry, for that was their real capacity—had commenced that southward race which was destined to become a laughable incident in history, Hamish and his confidence parted company.

Whereas he had once been staunch to the Hanoverian cause, he now considered that his worldly wealth would be more secure beneath the Stuart emblem. In a word, Hamish changed his allegiance.

This act synchronised with the sudden descent of Mrs. Harding on Lochavon—a happening that occurred some time before the battle of Cockenzie, or Prestonpans.

Hamish had repented. Seeing it was no longer safe openly to declare Hanoverian sympathies, he deemed it just as unsafe to support his rather misguided love affair with General Harding's widow, especially since she still liked being known by her maiden name, and since rumours of her real profession of spy were current in the district.

Therefore Hamish changed his politics and his affections at the same time—and disinherited both Saul and his mother, in favour of the prodigal Alastair.

Of this Alastair knew nothing, but Hamish Macdonald's wife, a genius at her trade, discovered the will the night she returned, and that same night the mysterious disappearance of Hamish Macdonald was the talk of all in the locality who had not stolen away to join the blue bonnets.

These gossips had seen the closed carriage depart. Some one declared that they had heard a cry for help. Others that they had seen Hamish Macdonald in bonds—his white face peering through the window of the carriage. Anyhow, when the following morning dawned Lochavon House was tenantless—and empty of wealth.

If Hamish Macdonald had fallen amongst thieves there were others who had not. Bonnie Prince Charlie's cause had been taken to Scotland's heart, and day by day the friendly pibroch heralded the approach of new forces who had found inspiration in the victory over Cope at Prestonpans.

CHAPTER XXIII

THE SKIRL OF THE PIPES

It was towards the end of October of the year seventeen hundred and forty-five that England began to look with real alarm upon the clouds that gathered away north, and by that time preparations for a move south had been prepared by Bonnie Prince Charlie's staff.

Charlie's gloom had now disappeared. He felt that at last he was to have his own way in the settling of the strategy to be followed, and he knew in his heart that, to inspire his beloved Highlanders, a real forward movement was the first essential.

As for Alastair, at first he had blessed the inaction, because it was enabling Fiona's wound to heal, and there was hope that they would not be parted; but, as Fiona mended and finally grew quite well, and as yet no action had been taken to cross the border, Alastair grew morose and unhappy.

It needed all Fiona's cheery optimism and continual good humour to keep Alastair's spirits up.

Alastair was more gloomy than ever on this night of nights, for he had been thinking of his father and his home, and the thoughts hurt.

There were four of them in the little room of the wine house. Fiona, Alastair, Sir John Daveril and "Red Angus," and they had all been talking on the usual topic of future plans, when a noisy altercation without broke in upon their conversation.

They could hear a stern voice speaking in aggressive tones to some one who had apparently not been quick enough in moving out of a horse's way, and the weak and quavering reply suggested that the speaker was an old man.

With an angry cry Alastair sprang to his feet and, darting across the tiled floor, flung open the old oaken door, to reveal a ragged and ill-clad old man crouching back against the wall, whilst a black-browed, foreign-looking individual was raising a whip menacingly.

The whip never fell.

Like a streak of light Alastair sprang at the horseman and caught the descending whip. The thongs lashed him but the lad held the wrist in a vice-like grip, and he wrenched the whip from its owner.

"Coward!" cried the young Macdonald. "Come down and show your true mettle in a fair fight." The next instant Alastair had snatched a riding gauntlet from the man's grasp and flung it full in his face.

Without another word the lad turned to see what could be done for the old man.

The old fellow was shivering with nervousness. He looked half-starved; his feet were poking out of his worn boots, and his clothes were tattered and almost in shreds.

He was a sad contrast to the carefully-groomed Sir John, the bonnie-looking Fiona and the picturesque Angus, all bedight with target and claymore and white-cockaded bonnet.

The old man was mumbling something that Alastair could not hear, so he came nearer and bent his ear to catch the old fellow's words.

"The call came to me as well, laddie," whispered rather than spoke the old fellow. "I heard it, and I came; for he's landed, and a mon must be with the bonnie laddie. But there was duty to my kinsman first, so I followed him, and well that I did."

Alastair started back, and then, stretching out his hand, raised the old fellow's head.

"Kenneth—old Kenneth!" he said softly. "Come to fight for Charlie!"

The wanderer's eyes were tired and dull with fatigue and age, but now they lighted up.

"I knew I'd find ye, laddie," he said softly. "It was God's providence that made this cock-a-hoop horseman upbraid an old man. Don't waste good Scottish steel on such an one, laddie."

Alastair's cheeks were aflame with anger. If he had been enraged before at this hectic horseman ill-treating an old man he was doubly angry now.

"This is all a mystery, Kenneth," said Alastair quickly. "Get you into the wine shop here, whilst I pay your debt to this fellow, and I'll join you when I have taught him some manners."

With that Alastair turned, to find that the rider had dismounted.

Seeing that his opponent was but a lad, there was a confident expression in the man's eyes.

"I am at your service," he said with aggressive hauteur. The rider spoke with a thick accent that rather suggested the guttural. He was either German or Dutch. Alastair could not determine which.

The Macdonald bowed, and, as he did so, Sir John Daveril stepped towards the challenged man.

"If you will accept my services, sir?" he ventured.

"Red Angus," fire in his eyes, and his broad hand on his claymore, had moved next to Alastair, and if looks had been as sharp as steel, Alastair's opponent was spitted already.

Sir John Daveril did not speak again, but, handing the principal's reins to a frightened ostler, he led the way away from the wine shop in the direction of a clump of trees, and through the trees to where a little glade lay.

Alastair did not need courage, if he needed skill, and he was quite calm as he slipped off his coat and took Sir John Daveril's sword.

His own was a claymore, so, as Sir John's weapon and that of the stranger were of a kind, and as the stranger agreed to the idea, Alastair took his friend's rapier and saluted his opponent.

Alastair's opponent was very tall and inclined to thinness. His sallow expression and small eyes accentuated the sinister appearance of the man, and now in his eyes there was a cat-like look which bade Alastair be wary of subterfuge and cunning.

The swords had barely touched before Macdonald realised that here was no mean opponent. The man had a long reach and his agile legs moved perfectly either to thrust or parry. His whole poise was that of a man trained to swordsmanship.

For some little time the two fought without any noticeable advantage, save that it became apparent to Angus that soon the man would lose his temper.

Alastair, like Angus, saw that his man was growing impatient, so he sought to encourage the duellist's manner by a lunge forward and a quick parry, and a second lunge with which he managed to prick the arm of his antagonist.

A wince of pain crossed the man's face.

"So!" he whispered fiercely through clenched teeth. "You banter me, do you. At you, then, my fine young sir!"

Alastair made no reply. A red spot was growing on the white shirt of the opponent, and now he came at Alastair in a sudden fierce rally that drove the lad backward.

But the duellist seemed to encounter a forest of swords as he made that attack, and soon he found that the forward movement had been checked very abruptly, and it was as much as he could do to protect himself from the steel that threatened to pass his guard at any moment.

The man was panting; the touch on his sword arm had grown more painful, and the slender rapier felt heavy.

Alastair was following up his success, but his anxiety to finish the affair was responsible for his tripping and falling over a piece of uneven ground.

For one moment he seemed an easy victim, for with a snarl the duellist had shorted his sword for a vicious lunge downwards through the lad's shoulder, but, thanks to a quick wriggle, the thrust missed its objective and Alastair sprang back to his feet, as the man stumbled and fell.

He was now an easy prey to Alastair's sword, but that was not the lad's way.

Macdonald waited for him to come back to position, and then with cool confidence he began to drive him round and round until the fellow must have been dazed, and at last, with a lightning thrust and a quick turn, he sent his opponent's sword flying into the air and sought to withdraw his point, but the duellist, worn out, had collapsed on to it and buried his shoulder in the steel.

Sir John Daveril dashed forward and knelt by the man's

side, whilst Alastair drew his rapier through a tuft of grass.

The lad knew full well that the wound was more painful than serious, and in a moment later Sir John confirmed this.

"A neat and merciful thrust," he said. "It does you credit, for the man would have killed you even by foul means had the chance offered itself again after you stumbled."

"It is but a scratch," said Sir John, as he rose to his feet. "I believe that fright was responsible for the collapse— that wound would not make an average man swoon so deeply."

"What shall we do with him?" asked Angus.

"Leave him for a few minutes," said Sir John, "and then take him back to some lodging we will find for him."

Fiona turned to Alastair.

"You fought fairly and well, Alastair," she whispered, "and you have nothing to reproach yourself for."

"We must help him all we can now," said her cousin quickly. "If we knew his name it would serve us better."

He paused, and then, seeing a pile of papers fallen from the enemy's coat, he walked towards them and, bending down, picked them up.

"There can be no harm in finding out this way," he said —and then he paused . . .

"What's the matter, Macdonald . . . ?"

Alastair's eyes were full of excitement, but he did not speak in answer to Sir John's questions; instead, he extended a missive to him.

Sir John Daveril saw the written words and gazed with amazement at his friend.

"Fiona!" whispered Alastair. "Look at this, Fiona!"

The girl came to his side as slowly and with deliberation he read the following:

"Hunt Kenneth Macdonald to earth, as you would a fox, for he has the will and the letter to Hamish Macdonald's son. It is urgent and necessary that neither the will nor the letter should reach their destination."

And the letter was signed "Hannah Harding."

A gasp of astonishment came from Fiona's lips as her cousin read the short note, and her amazed eyes were full on Alastair's.

Sir John Daveril did not speak.

He was looking down at the silent figure of the man Macdonald had wounded, and contempt was writ large on every line of his face.

"A spy," he said at last. "And worse . . ."

Daveril came to Alastair's side.

Laying his hand on Macdonald's shoulder he looked deep into Alastair's eyes.

"This is a great discovery, in more ways than one, lad," he said softly. "It proves beyond the shadow of a doubt that Hamish Macdonald, my old friend, has come to his senses at last, and that he has been spirited away, so that his allegiance and his wealth should not be offered to our Prince's cause."

Alastair's eyes lit up.

"You believe that my father is loyal to the Stuart cause?" he asked eagerly.

"It seems so, Alastair," put in Fiona, "else this man's mission had not been necessary."

"Red Angus," a monument of silence as usual, was the only member of the little party paying attention to the fallen man, whose eyes were now opening.

As the stranger came back to consciousness, so just as speedily did he take in the situation. He saw his papers; then he looked intently at his late antagonist, and understood, and, with an angry exclamation, staggered to his feet.

He was not equal to such exertion and would have fallen back to the ground again had not "Red" run to him and held him.

"My papers!" exclaimed the man. "Is it not enough to inflict a wound upon me without spying on me as well?"

Angus laughed.

"The wound was of your own seeking," he said sternly. "And it seems that some of your papers concern us even more than they do you, the one in connection with Hamish Macdonald's will, for instance."

The man's face, pale already, grew livid from fear and surprise.

"What have *you* to do with Hamish Macdonald?" he asked quickly.

Angus smiled into the frightened eyes.

"Who knows?" he answered. "But whether I know little or whether I know a lot does not alter the fact that you ride for another King than the one we serve, and methinks your eyes are your chief asset."

"You babble, man," said the stranger weakly. "I am a traveller and no party to this civil war of yours."

"You will have every opportunity to prove that," said Sir John Daveril, fixing the man with a keen glance.

"Come now," continued Sir John, "you are our prisoner until you have proved the innocence of your mission to Edinburgh. Take him along, Angus. I think you can manage without our assistance."

"Red" did not even smile, he simply indicated to his prisoner that it would be well if he came quietly, and so Captain Gunter von Honingen was led back to Edinburgh.

CHAPTER XXIV

KENNETH'S STORY

THE red glow of the light from the fire flickered on four interested faces. It danced about the oaken panelling of the little wine shop and found a different expression on the visages of those four, who seemed so hale and hearty by comparison with the tired and bowed old figure seated by the fireside, rubbing his hands and looking into the flames, as if for inspiration.

"I heard the call, too!" whispered, rather than spoke, old Kenneth. "There was no need to send the message to me, for it came night after night in the music of the burn—as I told ye, laddie," turning to gaze at Alastair.

"Night after night the sound came, and I prepared and I watched my kinsman and tried to turn his heart to the right cause, but he would have none of me then, just as he would have none of ye, lad."

Fiona and Alastair exchanged glances. It was a glimpse behind the scenes of happenings after Hamish Macdonald's unfortunate marriage.

"Then you went, lad," said Kenneth, "and I was left alone, for Miss Macdonald here had gone as well, and still Hamish Macdonald's heart was unchanged.

"The reason was not hard to find. One night I was sent for, and told to clear off the estate; and I knew that while the voice was the voice of my kinsman, the command came from my kinsman's wife. I did not go. I waited, and I watched, and then came through the news of the landing and of the gathering of the clans. The heather was on fire, and I sent word to Hamish to tell him—and he bade me stay, but in the background."

There was a note of sadness in the old man's voice as he recalled those scenes.

"Every one had gone, save my kinsman and myself," he continued. "And now the red coats came and Hamish entertained them, and then they went and we heard rumours of victory for our cause. Hamish came to me by the burn; there in the dusk of the evening I spoke my heart and made him strong. He was all for going to join Bonnie Prince Charlie, but on the night of his decision he was borne away.

"I was torn between two desires," said old Kenneth. "To get to my Prince or to stand by my kinsman. I chose to stand by Hamish, as the day had gone well with my Prince, and I followed south in his wake."

The old man chuckled.

"She didn't know I followed. She didn't know that where they stayed *I* stayed, always watching and waiting for my time; and so I came to Derby, and it was at Derby that I managed to get into my kinsman's prison."

"Prison!" exclaimed Alastair, leaping to his feet.

"Aye, lad," said Kenneth. "Kept as securely as any prisoner ever was. But I found him, and he told me to come north with a will he had made. He feared for his life."

Kenneth paused and looked deep into the flames of the fire.

"The journey has not been without its adventures," he said softly. "There was an inn by Preston where they tried to rob me, but I got away in the night and tramped all the way to Carlisle. I suspect that yon Captain Honingen could tell me something about that, but my eyes are not too good and I could not say that he was concerned. So I have come north, and on my way I have laughed at the warnings. 'Prince Charles has landed!' They told me 'The barbarians are killing all the women and children. They are cannibals!'"

Kenneth looked up.

"And they didn't know that I was a barbarian too!" he said with a chuckle; "that I listened to their stories of 'Cope's defeat because it was music to my ears."

"And here I am at last," he said wearily, "with the will safe and sound; and I want to help to rescue your father from his prison, for he has come back to the cause."

His story ended, Kenneth extended his hands to the blaze. It was the first cold night of early autumn, and without the wind was howling and shaking the old sign of the wine shop on its rusty hinges.

There was not one of the four listeners but eyed the old man with admiration, for they could realise all he had gone through.

Macdonald rose from his chair and walked over to Kenneth.

"What can I say in thanks, Kenneth?" he said quietly. "You have done more than was humanly possible, and I know that all of it has been too much for you."

Kenneth laughed.

"There is not much that is too much for a Macdonald," he answered. "But let us hope, lad, there will be much of that to become yours when you are Lochavon's chief."

With that Kenneth drew a long document from his pocket and handed it to Alastair.

"The will," he said, shortly.

He had barely spoken when, from without, there came the sudden tapping of drums and the silvery note of trumpets, followed by the sound of pipes and the even tramp of men marching in order.

Sir John Daveril moved to the door and opened it. A gust of wind blew into the room; and the light flickered and then fell on the cobbled way without.

And, as they watched that midnight spectacle the night became loud with the skirl of pipes and the thunder of marching men.

Alastair had come to Sir John's side.

"What does it mean?" he asked quickly.

Sir John smiled a high smile.

"The advance south has begun," he said, with a light in his eyes.

CHAPTER XXV

OVER THE BORDER

THE autumn mists, rising from the fields at morn, or sweeping down upon them at eve, saw the roads that led through them and to the border busy with the lumbering wagons and the sturdy Highland feet.

Watch fires in wood and coppice; vedettes cantering back with news of the clear way; and the music of Scotia's fearful pipes.

Marching south! South with Charlie! South with the Camerons, Mackenzies, Macdonalds, Gordons, Stewarts and MacLeods! South with such leaders as Tullibardine, Murray, Lochiel, Perth and many another whose names alone could stir the hearts of men to acts of supreme devotion and unutterable heroism.

South, after the years of peace! Back to the border and to win back the crown that once a James had brought from Dunedin to link two countries nearer the one to the other.

Was it wonderful that Government trembled?

Men's hearts were closed books those days, and could Charlie have opened them he would have found, in countless cases, brave reading for any gay Chevalier.

News from the north was being borne south by tired horses and stern-lipped riders, and the lips of Tullibardine's advance touched England at Reddington, while the western division of Charlie's army flowed over into the promised land.

But time had been wasted. And away in other lands the advance was having effect. Urgent orders were bringing soldiers back from Flanders, till London began thoroughly to appreciate the danger when the news was bruited abroad that six thousand Dutch troops were on their way to help bolster up the child of Orange.

So other roads were busy with feet. On to Newcastle went the hastily-collected army, and with it went Field-Marshal Wade, and Cumberland was being called home to his destiny.

Penrith, Kendal, Lancaster, Preston and Wigan passed into Charlie's hands. Sanguine hopes that the army would grow in strength with each day it advanced were dying as dreams die, for hardly a recruit came to the bonnie banner, and in Staffordshire another army was massing to do battle when occasion should arise.

Daveril shook his head as, with Alastair, he rode in the van towards Manchester.

"I do not like the signs," he said. "At Lancaster they blew kisses to the Prince and I honestly believe that they admired him; but somehow they seemed to know something of which we are ignorant."

"That they love the Prince and respect the way in which his loyal followers conduct themselves I have no doubt but their wisdom is deeper than their feelings, I am thinking, and we may live to realise that our feeling is no trumpet blast that can level a Hanoverian Jericho."

Alastair laughed gaily. "I always thought we were grave in the north, Sir John, but I really think that for dourness you can't beat a southern gentleman!"

Daveril had to smile, for Alastair's cheery optimism had kept his spirits up on many occasions when he fancied the cause doomed by too much dallying; and now the boy's mood had charmed his misgivings away.

"You are right," he said, "we do our Prince small service if we fear the future, and our hearts can swell with pride as we see with whom we march."

Alastair turned back and followed the direction of Sir John's glance.

As far as his eye could see moved line after line of marching men.

With the sun on the many-coloured kilts, shining on muskets and claymores, came Charlie's host. Alastair could see ridge after ridge of clansmen topping the hill and flowing forward like some swift-flowing blue stream, and the bonnets of the marchers completed the comparison.

Once the sun found the shining barrels of Cope's captured cannon.

It was a brave sight, and for some moments afterwards even Sir John Daveril's heart was full of hope.

Manchester provided further encouragement. There was no hindrance to the advance at the gates of that city, for it had already been seized on Prince Charlie's behalf before the blue bonnets were sighted. Nay, more, when, to the merry sound of fife and drum, the Highlanders swung into the streets they were met with real cheers, and their coming was responsible for the enlisting of three hundred men.

Alastair's hopes were high, and he would have been the happiest individual on the world had not one very important thing weighed upon his mind.

His father!

Kenneth had been left in the north when the advance had commenced, but before their parting the old man had implored Alastair to hasten to his father's rescue.

Now, during the weary march Alastair had chafed at all delays, congested roads, deflections from the main route, missions back to keep communication with other regiments and all the hundred and one things that were part of his duty as an officer in the service of the Prince.

Clanranald's counsels to Bonnie Prince Charlie had not gone unheeded, and by reason of this Alastair was given work of real responsibility and deeply trusted.

But at Manchester he found a respite from his staff duties,

and at Manchester he decided that by hook or by crook he would get to Derby.

He mentioned the matter to Daveril.

"If I waited any longer, Sir John," he said, "I verily believe that I should go mad. It seems years since Kenneth came with news of my father and even now I may be too late to render him any service."

Sir John agreed with the urgency of the matter and promised his help in the obtaining of leave for Alastair; but fortunately for Macdonald his good offices were not needed, for that same night Lord George Murray sent for Alastair.

The massive and somewhat repulsive face of the leader was raised from glancing at a letter he had been writing as Alastair entered the plainly-furnished room where he sat.

"Ah!" he said in a rough voice. "Macdonald—good."

He eyed Alastair sternly, as though he was weighing up all Macdonald's points and forming his own opinion of the lad's usefulness.

"I have heard that you have uses," he said at last. Alastair bowed.

"I have served my kinsman of Clanranald and Glenaladale," he replied in even tones. Lord George had a way of hectoring a man that made some nervous of him, but as Alastair looked into that ugly face he saw beyond the harshness of it and realised the responsibility that rested upon this Highlander.

"It was Clanranald advised me to employ you," said Murray. "Said you could be trusted, had good luck, and were handy with your weapons—am I right or wrong?"

"One could not properly serve Prince Charles if they did not possess such good fortune and usual virtues," answered Alastair quietly.

"I believe you," said Lord George. He eyed Alastair carefully.

"Get you off to Derby to-night," he said sharply. "Seek

out Macintyre at an inn called The Three Tuns, try to learn all the movements you can with regard to the army at Lichfield, and prepare the way for our coming, or warn us if we seem in danger of being trapped, for there are far too many opportunities for traps to my liking."

"I will ride at once," said Alastair.

But Lord George Murray did not hear, for he had turned again to his letter.

CHAPTER XXVI

THE HOUSE WITH THE UNLIGHTED WINDOWS

THESE days the citizens of Derby had other things to talk of; but time was, and not so many days back, when the house of so many mysterious happenings had been a matter of real interest and deep speculation.

They call it "The House with the Unlighted Windows," and at night they passed it by, as though some evil spirit dwelt there.

The house was mystic and evil, and none knew what happened there, although some declared that the devil held the place in thrall and used it as his headquarters in Derby.

Once some bold spirits had decided to pay a visit to the house, and they had managed to gain access to the place, only to be driven back with fear in their hearts by a most direful scream that had echoed amidst the rafters and had gone chasing out into the night like some released evil spirit.

After that they had been less venturesome, and the house had been given a wide berth.

But if on this October day eyes could have peered through the dusty panes of one of the upper windows they would have seen something that would have occasioned supreme surprise and banished for ever the report that the place was obsessed.

Lying on some straw in the far corner of the room, and with his wrists and ankles shackled, was an ill-clad, emaciated man.

His hair was matted and a straggly white beard gave him the appearance of some wild man of the sea. A tattered shirt was open at the throat and revealed his skinny arms.

No one would have recognised the once trim and keen-eyed Hamish Macdonald in this pathetic object with the sagging jaws and dirty appearance. But Hamish Macdonald it was, and he had suffered greatly since he had turned Alastair adrift on the world.

Days of living death and sleepless nights had found him thinking of all that Alastair had said. He had seen his son with different eyes and had remembered Alastair's scathing condemnation of Saul and Saul's mother, and now he knew how right the boy had been in all he had said.

And Hamish was holding out grimly now, just as a city holds out; and he was holding out for Alastair's sake.

"You may keep me captive, break my health—kill me," he had said to Mrs. Harding and his jailer, Rustler. "But you shall not rob my son of his inheritance, for I know that you lied against him. I know that it was you who caused the rift between us."

The lack-lustre eyes of Hamish Macdonald looked up suddenly. From without his prison there had come the sound of footsteps, and an eager light now took the place of the dull stare. It was an incident in the day, an event, when Rustler came with his meagre meal of bread and cheese and water.

A rusty key grated in a rustier lock, and the door was opened to reveal on the threshold of the little, low-ceilinged room, one of the most repulsive creatures the eye could possibly see.

Rustler's eyes were small and squinted evilly, and his head was bullet-shaped and partly bald, although what hair there was upon it was long. Black wisps of coarse hair fell across his forehead.

But the man's figure was the most noticeable thing. Rustler's legs were bowed and tremendous in girth and his shoulders were the shoulders of a giant. The ugly head seemed just fastened on them, as though put there as an afterthought.

He clumped into the room and eyed his captive.

"Well," he said grimly. "Do you feel more in a mind to sign the paper? We've pampered you too long, I would have dealt otherwise with you long since."

"You have done much," said Hamish. "What further ill-treatment could you inflict?"

Rustler's already narrow eyes narrowed even more and a nasty glint came into them.

"Some pretty things," he murmured; "wring that signature from you with the terror of the flame and the thumb-screw. Pretty tortures, my fine Scot."

"That would not make me do a thing I had decided not to do," said Hamish. "I have suffered so much at your hands that torture would be a welcome change to this dreadful monotony."

A strange look came into Rustler's eyes.

"Not when the pain comes," he said wickedly. "Not when one is in agony. The mind cannot fight against torture, for I know—I have seen it time and again."

He came nearer to Hamish and leant over him, so that his hot breath fell on Macdonald's face.

"You shall know what it is to-night," he said. "And to-night you shall sign, for we have waited long enough."

With that he raised himself and clumped towards the door. The next moment he had left the room, the door was closed behind him and the sound of a woman's voice interrogating Rustler reached Macdonald's ears.

Meanwhile, in another part of Derby a very different scene could have been witnessed.

With the froth about its nostrils a horse had come to

a standstill outside the inn known as The Three Tuns, and a young gentleman, clad in the typical dress of the landed classes, lowered himself wearily from the saddle and threw the reins to an ostler who had come from the stables at the sound of horse's hoofs on the cobbled yard.

The newcomer found the inn empty. Although the sun was shining fitfully none of its light was imparted to the interior of this old-fashioned hostelry, and the only light that illuminated the little hall came from a cheery fire that crackled in a room at the end of it.

The place was empty, but the sound of approaching footsteps told him that his arrival had been noticed by others beside the ostler.

A tall and broad figure blocked the entrance to the room, and the flickering firelight, shining on his face, showed it to be a ruddy-coloured and pleasing visage.

The rider looked carefully at him. The man smiled and came into the room.

"Your wishes, sir?" he asked.

"I have ridden far," came the peculiar reply, "and the roads are dusty this dry weather."

He paused.

"Heather burns these days," he added, glancing keenly at the man who had asked his wishes.

The man now looked behind him, to see if any other customers had entered the inn and, apparently satisfied that he was not being overheard, he coughed discreetly and then closed the door—and locked it.

"It is on fire," came his answer. "You have come from Lord George Murray?"

"Yes," was the sharp answer. "My name is Alastair Macdonald, and I bear this letter to you from Lord George."

Seating himself on a chair, Alastair slipped off one of his riding boots and drew a letter from the boot. The man took it with eager fingers.

"I am Macintyre," he said shortly.

CHAPTER XXVII

THE TABLES TURNED

THE fading light of the short October day had never seemed so grim to Hamish Macdonald.

The courage of the past had been sorely tried, and the stern resolution to keep strong and to his word had been weakened by weeks of suffering and loneliness.

Night was approaching and with the night Rustler would carry out his threat, and with a sinking heart Hamish realised that he would need to be almost superhuman not to give way to weakness.

In the distance he could hear a clock sounding the hours with a grim monotony.

One — two — three — four — five — six — seven — eight —nine.

Ten.

Hamish Macdonald heard a footstep on the stairs. Then there came the sound of voices, and the grating of the key in the lock.

The door opened and the faint ray of a shaded lantern shone in on the room.

Some one crossed the floor with a quick step and hung a black curtain in front of the window, and then the light was turned upon Hamish Macdonald.

It almost blinded him at first.

With difficulty he looked into it, but at last he was able to see the figures of Rustler and his wife.

She was standing by the door with a malevolent look on her face.

"I hope you are going to see reason at last," she said abruptly.

"What do you mean?" asked Hamish, turning in her direction.

"Sign the will in Saul's favour, and you shall go free to join that precious Prince Charlie of yours," said the woman bitterly.

Hamish laughed. It was the travesty of a laugh and it echoed strangely through the prison chamber.

"Not if you torture me a thousand times," said Hamish Macdonald quickly. "You lied about Alastair all the time you were playing a part. You came north to spy on the activities of the Chiefs and now you would have me sign away my son's birthright. No, a thousand times no!"

Mrs. Harding's florid face grew even more florid, and she raised her hand as though she was about to dash forward and strike the man whose life she had done her best to ruin.

"You will sign!" she cried. "Rustler shall see that you sign. I have lost patience with you. There shall be no mercy now."

Rustler meanwhile had not been idle.

With the window carefully veiled from the view of those who wandered through Derby's darkened streets, he was busying himself with heating some pokers.

Rustler, an expert at torture, had brought up a little brazier and now the pokers were beginning to glow amid the coals.

It fascinated the eyes of Hamish. Those glowing coals seemed like critical eyes that watched him, and, in foolishness of mind, he began to wonder what the pokers were for.

He was growing light-headed. At times he wanted to break into uncontrollable laughter, but each time that the feeling came he steadied himself; but he still watched the glowing fire and waited for what would happen.

At last Rustler was satisfied that his tools were ready for work.

Drawing one of the pokers out of the brazier he motioned to Mrs. Harding.

She came forward and glowered down at Hamish Macdonald.

"You've one chance left," she said in a low voice. "Sign and win your liberty, or refuse to sign and prepare to have the signature forced from you."

A wan smiled flickered across the face of Hamish Macdonald.

"You do not terrify me," he said. "Better death than this existence, and in death I do know that my son's inheritance is safe."

"Sign—I command it!" she cried.

"I refuse!" he answered.

Mrs. Harding swung round on Rustler.

"Then make him sign," she cried. "There is no way with some fools, and, as he doesn't value his life, let him be taught the value of it."

Rustler wasted no time.

With a red hot poker in each hand he approached his victim, and he saw with delight that Hamish Macdonald shuddered as the red-hot objects were waved in front of his eyes.

Hamish cowered back.

"So you are afraid!" scoffed Rustler. "I thought these would make you see reason."

"Take them away! Take them away!" cried Hamish. His last strength had gone. Never a strong man, he had done more than was expected of him, and now his moral courage had gone.

"Not so quickly," said Rustler. "Will you sign?"

A last despairing fight was going on in Hamish's breast. He looked up with an agonised expression at Rustler—an expression which was wasted.

"No!" he cried, and with that the last vestive of colour drained from his face and he fell forward in a dead faint.

"Bring the fool to," said Mrs. Harding harshly.

With a muttered imprecation, Rustler took the pokers back and placed them in the brazier and sought, with the help of the bottle of water at Macdonald's side, to bring him back to consciousness.

It was no easy task.

Hamish, weakened by hunger and ill-usage, lay limp in Rustler's grasp.

The man fancied him dead, but the flicker of Macdonald's eyelids told him that the victim still lived, and at last Macdonald opened his eyes and looked into those of his torturer.

"Let me die!" he moaned. "Let me die!"

"Not so fast," said Rustler. "Sign that paper, and then die if you like. But sign that paper."

"I will not sign!" said Hamish.

Rustler let Macdonald fall back against the wall, and the next moment slipped his hand into one of his large pockets and withdrew an object that, with a deft movement, he forced on Macdonald's thumb.

He began to screw it until Macdonald cried out with agony, but even then Rustler did not cease.

"I'll sign," cried Hamish at last. "Give me the paper. I'll sign!"

Rustler unscrewed the instrument of torture from Macdonald's thumb as Mrs. Harding, a picture of excitement and anticipation, came forward with a paper upon which something was written in a man's handwriting.

Mrs. Harding handed a pen to Hamish.

Then she found some ink and, with feverish eyes, she watched him dip the pen in the ink and prepare to sign the document.

Hamish raised the pen, and, as he did so, from below, in the well of the house, there came a thunderous knocking.

"What's that?"

It was Rustler who spoke and, trembling in every limb, he dashed to the window.

"Sign!" hissed Mrs. Harding.

Hamish did not make any attempt to do so. Instead, he listened again for that knocking. It had somehow inspired him with a new courage and now he threw the pen away with an exclamation.

"I will *not* sign!" he cried.

Rustler came back from the window, and brandished a red-hot poker before Macdonald's eyes.

"Sign—and quickly!" he ordered.

From below the banging on the door was growing in intensity, and now Mrs. Harding gave a cry.

Suddenly there came a reverberating crash and a cry from below—the sound of footsteps on the stairs.

"The door, fool!" she cried to Rustler. The door . . ."

Rustler dashed towards the door, and in his anxiety to close it dropped the poker on to the heap of straw where Hamish Macdonald lay.

He was too late to bar the entry of four figures.

Alastair Macdonald, rapier in hand, followed by Macintyre and two other men—friends of the innkeeper—had rushed into the room.

Alastair fell full tilt upon Rustler and sent him flying into a corner, where he lay silent and momentarily stunned.

Mrs. Harding had fallen to the floor in a swoon, and busy hands were tearing Hamish Macdonald away from the spreading flames.

Macintyre carried a hammer—he had burst the door in with this—and now this hammer was useful to smash Hamish's fetters.

They fell apart as Hamish collapsed—utterly worn out.

Macintyre picked him up in his strong arms and bore him down the stairs, followed by Alastair and his two comrades.

Hamish had been the first consideration, and, with him once in the safety of the street, the two turned back to get Mrs. Harding.

Alastair returned with them and managed to get to the second floor just as Rustler came down the stairs and through the smoke.

He was alone, but a few minutes later from above there

came a cry, and, ringed about by flames, Mrs. Harding appeared.

Alastair tore above to her assistance, through the smoke and the flames.

CHAPTER XXVIII

THE NIGHT OF SURPRISE

TERROR had unnerved Mrs. Harding, and now, uncertain of which direction to take, she stood amid the smoke, whilst the flames from the now-thoroughly-ignited room came licking with angry and evil tongues towards her.

Alastair had realised her danger at once, and now he was by her side and shouting to her to make some attempt to dare the stairs. He caught at the woman's arm and dragged her from the landing and below, and so came to the smoke-clouded hall just as the upper stairs collapsed in a burning heap.

Now the cool wind was blowing on Alastair's face and the burning house towered up above them. He had dragged Mrs. Harding out into a street that was filled with people, but Macintyre was nowhere to be seen and Macintyre's friends had become one with the night.

And Mrs. Harding was regaining her senses.

Alastair's first thoughts were for his father; but Hamish Macdonald had disappeared just as mysteriously as Macintyre. It seemed apparent to Alastair that, knowing he was safe, knowing that he had gained the street, they had made off to give Hamish shelter.

The wisdom of this move was soon to become apparent.

As the crowd of people saw the boy and the woman leave the fog of smoke that was issuing from the old building they gave a cheer, and soon the two were ringed about by jostling prentices and excited citizens come to enjoy this sensation of a fire as a relief after all the talk of war and Prince Charlie's approach to their city.

Mrs. Harding had regained her senses with remarkable rapidity.

The dazed and wild-eyed woman of a moment or so since had changed into the astute and keen-faced creature who had held Hamish Macdonald in thrall and had sent his son into the world, penniless.

If Alastair had expected her to join in the chorus of praise that was being showered upon him by the crowd he was vastly disappointed. Mrs. Harding, still choking somewhat from the effects of the smoke, surveyed him with a green and glistening eye and a dangerous curl wreathed itself in her thin lips—but she did not speak.

Alastair sought to elbow his way through the crowd that hemmed him in, but it was not to be. They were for lifting him on their shoulders as a sign of their appreciation. Their cheers still rang above the crackle of the flames.

A sensation-loving and volatile crowd! They could have guffawed with as much unison and ease as they cheered, they could have condemned just as quickly as they praised; and this fact was shortly to be proved and in dramatic fashion.

Suddenly, there came a lull in the cheering, and evidently it afforded Mrs. Harding the opportunity for which she had been waiting.

Raising her head, and eyeing the crowd, she pointed an accusing finger at Alastair.

"Do not be mistaken," she cried. "Do not waste your cheers on a Jacobite spy—he came to make me a prisoner, not to save my life, and others came with him, but they have made good their escape. See to it that this ones does not escape you, for he has come to sell your city to the Highland wolves who, before long, will be growling at your gates!"

Mrs. Harding had a gift of oratory and her words certainly had some effect with the mob, for now a dead silence followed, and the eyes of the crowd were gazing at the slim figure of Alastair.

The blood had left Macdonald's face. He stood there hardly believing his ears. This ingratitude had stunned him as though it were a blow from a heavy hand, and he remained there dazed and unbelieving that he had heard the words at all.

A stone struck Alastair's bonnet from his head. It was followed by the groan of a man—struck by another thrown from behind Alastair.

"Into the fire with him!" shouted a loud-voiced harridan.

"Club him!" cried a man.

A face leered into Alastair's eyes. Two brutal eyes gleamed into his own and two strong hands caught him as in a vice.

"Traitor!" said an evil voice. "Jacobite spy!"

Alastair sought to extricate himself from the grasp, but he failed to get away from those pinioning arms, and he knew that the man was determined.

Rustler had returned, and was making the capture for the crowd.

"Take him to the City Hall!" cried a man near Rustler, and the crowd took the suggestion up. "To the City Hall with him!" they shouted, and they made way for Rustler as, despite Alastair's struggles, they forced him along.

Above them the windows were opened, and every street was adding new recruits to the crowd which by now had become enormous.

Garbage, bricks, tins, anything that the rowdy element could lay its hands on began to hurtle through the air.

Alastair had been struck on the head, and was feeling sick and dizzy as he stumbled along in Rustler's grip.

Down this street, up that street, jostled here and buffeted there, Alastair was drawn nearer and nearer to the town hall.

Runners had informed the mayor of their coming, and the burghers of the city had been warned that something was amiss, for the whole of Derby was seething with some strange excitement.

Torches had been procured, and the Mayor of Derby waiting for the coming of this strange procession, saw a vast multitude thrown into relief by the light of flambeaux, and as he heard the cries of the crowd he realised that something of importance was toward.

And away in the background of the crowd . . .

With Hamish Macdonald safely within The Three Tuns, Macintyre and his trusted friends had sallied out again in search of Alastair, and attracted by the noise and the torches, had seen what was happening.

Macintyre looked grave. With the mob in such a mood he did not hold out much hope in his own heart for the life of the gallant boy who had come to him from Lord George Murray.

He realised the hopelessness of the position, the futility of attempting rescue, with only three against all these masses of people.

Alastair's senses were numbed now. He vaguely remembered being forced by Rustler to the foot of the City Hall steps. He saw some armed citizens behind an elderly man. He felt himself gripped by other arms than Rustler's and distantly heard the old man crying to the mob that the law must be observed and the prisoner tried according to the law.

Then Alastair heard the deafening disagreement of the crowd.

A woman was encouraging them. Her accusing hand was first pointed at Alastair and then at the old man, the mayor. Alastair heard her strident voice shouting for a rope, and he realised at once that it was his step-mother's.

He composed himself. Gradually the old calm returned to him, and he raised his head with dignity and looked with contempt at the shouting, murderous mob. They would cry differently when the advance came south and the news was told to Lord George Murray.

The crowd had expected to see him cringe before their first citizen; they had waited for his cry of mercy; but neither cringing nor appeal was to add to their amusement.

The mayor, with a pathetic gesture to the guards who had come within, stepped back into the shadows of the City Hall. He did not want to see this unlawful sight. He respected the law and was sick at heart that his respect and judgment had been overruled by an apparently demented multitude.

Rustler was again Alastair's gaoler. Rustler's hands had fitted the rope, and now, with help, they were dragging Alastair to where an inn sign rattled in the wind above the heads of the crowd.

The inn was closed, but a ruddy light fell from an open window on the boy's features, and found them unafraid.

Discretion had made mine host open one of the doors to let in the man with the rope, and now this man, leaning out of the window, flung the end of the rope over the iron arm that held the sign.

Whilst eager hands made the rope taut, others took off the first halter that had been wound about Alastair's neck and tied his arms with it, and then the new noose was slipped over his head. He was gripped by two of Rustler's assistants, whilst Rustler himself prepared to launch Alastair into eternity.

A strange silence had come over the crowd now. They seemed to realise that they were in the presence of death, and also in the presence of a very brave lad, who stood beneath the light with nothing on his face that betrayed fear or other than supreme contempt for his captors.

CHAPTER XXIX

AT THE ELEVENTH HOUR

MACINTYRE, white-lipped and fearful for the lad beneath the lamp, turned to his two friends.

"Towards the inn," he whispered to Clarkson, one of his friends. "It is the only chance we have."

His friends followed, as Macintyre, not sparing to be rough, forced himself through the press of people.

They let Macintyre pass until he was nearly at the inn. His arrival was timed just as the man who had carried the rope above was leaving the inn, but Macintyre prevented the landlord locking and closing the door.

The landlord made way, for there was something in Macintyre's eyes that commanded obedience, and so Macintyre came within the inn, and Clarkson, and Jobling, his friends, with him.

"Bolt and bar the door," cried Jobling to Clarkson, "then mount with Mac."

Clarkson wasted no time, but did as he was bidden, and then, drawing his pistol from his pocket, dashed after the other two. He entered the upper room to see a strange thing.

The innkeeper and his two daughters and a serving maid were standing terrified in a corner, where Jobling was holding them up with two loaded horse-pistols.

Macintyre was on the carved iron balcony just above Alastair's head.

"I tell you," he cried, "that this man is mine. I have a score to settle with the spy. Let him come above, and I'll toss him down to you."

The crowd murmured.

"String him up!" came a shout. "We are tired of this waiting. Let the spy swing!"

"He's my man, I tell you," cried Macintyre. "Hand him over or . . ."

It was then that Rustler, growing accustomed to the light as he looked upward, recognised one of those who had figured in the rescue of Hamish Macdonald.

"He's another spy!" he cried. "That man up there is an impostor and a friend of this fellow we have here. Let's string this one up and then get the others from the inn!"

A cry of approval greeted this short speech, and an ominous movement was made towards Alastair.

A look of desperation had wreathed itself about Macintyre's lips.

"Come a step forward," he cried, "and I'll blow daylight through ye."

Dead silence followed his words and then a nervous movement at the back of the crowd suggested that some of the less valorous onlookers were making for home. A woman—seeing the light glinting on the barrels of Macintyre's pistols—screamed. The crowd swayed this way and that. Those who were too near Alastair tried to get back, but those who pressed forward to watch sent them a degree nearer the now hopeful Macdonald.

"Back, ye hounds," cried Macintyre. "Back, I say!"

He leapt over and pointed the pistol at Rustler.

"Drop that rope, or you die now," he said grimly.

Rustler did not move. He thought it a bluff, but he knew his mistake the next moment, for Macintyre's pistol spoke, and Rustler fell at the feet of his victim, and there was a gaping wound in Rustler's shoulder.

Hastily Macintyre reloaded his pistol and waited.

"Any one else brave enough to come forward!" he cried. "Touch that rope any of you and you share that fellow's fate or worse."

A tremble of terror took the crowd in its grip. It was just as easy to make them afraid as it had been to arouse their ugly passions, and now those in front were terribly afraid of those two pistols and of the two pistols in the hands of the man who stood just behind Macintyre.

"What was that . . .?"

A man had spoken to another man in the crowd. Alastair heard his words, and he heard the crowd take them up.

"Drums!"

Some one shrieked, and then there came a great cry from the distance and the sound of racing feet.

And then . . .

Above the cries of the crowd, above the sound of their feet, as they strove to get into the side streets, there came the skirl of the pipes and the loud roll of drums and the shouts of marching men.

With a sigh on his lips, and with the rope still about his neck, Alastair fell forward.

"Quick!" said Macintyre to Clarkson. "Get below and release him, whilst I wait here and watch events."

Jobling had lowered his horse-pistols as Clarkson ran below and to the street.

Clarkson severed Alastair's bonds and picked the lad up in his strong arms and bore him into the hostelry.

Glory shone in Macintyre's eyes now, for the Prince for whom he had waited so long had come, Hamish Macdonald had been rescued, and Alastair's life had been spared.

He had placated the innkeeper by explaining what had occurred, and had promised to speak well to Bonnie Prince Charlie's leaders of the innkeeper, so mine host realised that instead of having fallen in with thieves he had been the unconscious means of preserving himself and his family from the wild Scotsmen who lived like wolves and had been so evilly reported upon.

There was no doubt that the Prince had come, for even then his drums were rousing glorious echoes and the timorous city folk, quick to change their attitude, were acclaiming his gallant-looking troops.

Derby had fallen with only one casualty, and that casualty was Rustler, who had died as he had lived—like a rat, and in a gutter.

CHAPTER XXX

CRITICAL DAYS

ALASTAIR had taken Macintyre to Lord George, and had seen Murray and explained the happenings since Macdonald's arrival in Derby.

"General Wade is marching hard, sir," said Alastair, "and my Lord of Cumberland is at Stafford. I have this on good authority."

Lord George Murray's brows narrowed.

"They are over thirty thousand strong," he said grimly, "and we are but a paltry five."

Glenaladale and Clanranald, standing behind Murray, exchanged glances.

"What says Prince Charles?" asked Clanranald quickly.

Murray smiled.

"At last he appreciates the significance of this mad adventure," he said bitterly. "I, too, was at fault, as indeed we all were. We might have known that rumour was a lying jade and that no such number of loyal Jacobites as that which was anticipated would flock to our standard."

"Do we fight?" It was Glenaladale who spoke.

Lord George Murray did not answer; from the gloom of the room a figure had appeared.

It was Lochiel.

"Fight!" he exclaimed. "Do you mean to retire now that we have come so far? True, we are few against many, but was the advantage on our side at Prestonpans? Must we seem poltroons, cowards in the sight of Wade and Cumberland when we laughed so at Cope and Cope's cowardice?"

It was the honest outburst of a very gallant soldier, but not the speech of a strategist.

Murray smiled indulgently and looked at the Cameron.

"You speak as I feel, Lochiel," he said with quiet firmness, "but this is no lottery, to stake all on one throw. We have deceived Cumberland once; we must deceive him again. We have left our own homes open to the ravages of a Duke whose reputation for brutality was a byword in Flanders. We only gain ground by advancing—not victories—and meanwhile troops are massing between us and our own country. If we fight let it be on ground of our own choosing —not a trap and between two fires."

He paused.

"Wade, as young Macdonald here has told you, is coming up by hard marches by the east road and an army as large as his lies between us and London. Three armies to one. We should be mad to fight against such odds!"

Lochiel moved away. He would have rather stood the ordeal of battle than the ordeal of telling his men that their advance had been stayed, and that with the dawn the column would be marching back by the way it had come.

"That will do, Macdonald," said Murray to Alastair. "You have done good service, and you will continue to do so if you remain silent upon what you have heard here. Report to Sir John Daveril."

Alastair bowed and withdrew, leaving Scotia's chieftains to one of the saddest moments of their lives.

The army was full of high spirits when at last it commenced its march out of Derby. The Highlanders marched, thinking that it was to battle, but when the news ran down the line that battle would not be joined until more favourable circumstances were met with, all grew sullen and silent.

They marched with lowered heads and men hardly dared glance at their fellows, for Scottish pride had come low, and that was a bad thing.

If Prince Charles's advance had been clever his retreat was a masterpiece of generalship. By intricate and subtle manœuvre, by quick, forced marches, by dexterous suggestions of false moves Cumberland was deceived, and his following force of cavalry and mounted infantry found the going harder than the lithe mountain children who followed a laughing Prince.

The retreat had not damped his gay spirits.

It is always more difficult to retreat than to advance, and it should have been made more difficult still by the actions of the inhabitants upon the line of march, but they, remembering the chivalry of the past, repaid in kind, and it is on record that Cumberland was met with a deal less civility than were those ragged but lion-hearted sons of Scotland who trudged back towards the border.

Cumberland was pursuing with all the speed he could command, and Alastair, who was attached to Lord George Murray's command, was acting with Sir John Daveril in keeping in touch with Cumberland's cavalry.

"My sword arm itches, Alastair," said Sir John, as he and Alastair sat talking at Shap.

Some wagons had broken down, and the artillery had been delayed, so all the available mounted infantry and cavalry had been deputed to watch and wait, in case Cumberland's cavalry should make a lightning stroke.

"You mean a fight is near?" asked Alastair.

Sir John laughed.

"I have it in my blood," he answered. "What is that?"

Daveril sprang to his feet, for a silvery note had rung out, and Sir John's troop were hastening to their horses.

Alastair and Sir John mounted and rode towards the troop, to find it surrounding a wounded rider who reeled in his saddle.

"On our flanks!" exclaimed the man. "Clouds of cavalry!"

Then suddenly came the sound of a fusillade.

CHAPTER XXXI

A TASTE OF SCOTTISH STEEL

"CLOUDS OF CAVALRY on both flanks, and Cumberland's army cutting off our line of retreat!"

Sir John Daveril and Alastair Macdonald listened to the words of the wounded man. He was not of the army. A sympathiser with the Jacobite cause, he had risked everything to bear the tidings of the approaching thunder-clouds, and in so doing had found a mortal wound.

Having spoken he fell forward on his horse. He had given his all for the Prince who had passed his way!

Now, over the lip of the rolling hills, carried by the crisp morning breeze, came the clear-throated call of the cavalry trumpet.

The cloud of depression had vanished like a mist at sun-up. No longer were the faces of Murray's, Perth's and Lochiel's men downcast and sad. A whip lash could not have stirred any single man of that retreating army so much as Cumberland's shrill little trumpets that spoke so confidently to the morning skies.

Sir John Daveril's troop, wheeling off the road, was galloping out on the right flank.

Fiona, unrecognisable now, for she was clad as Alastair was clad and armed as Alistair was armed—rode at her cousin's side.

Grim-lipped they rode forward, banking up. Cumberland's cavalry was advancing upon the Duke of Perth's infantry and already a fusillade told that action had been joined.

Sir John's gentlemen had been joined by two other troops, and now the Duke of Perth's Highlanders, deploying from the road, opened fire on the advancing cavalry.

But between Sir John and Perth's men, with a jangling of harness and a sheen of swords, some hundred cavalrymen were riding, with intent to get behind that dogged little force that seemed undismayed at the appearance of Cumberland's horse.

"Ride close to me, Fiona," said Alastair to his cousin. "In a moment we shall be charging their flank, for see, already Perth's men are driving back the frontal attack, and our opportunity has come to break the order of these over-daring riders in front of us."

Fortune, in the guise of powder smoke and morning mist, undulating land and scrub, had concealed the coming of Daveril's horsemen.

They now breasted a little ridge, and before them, preparing to wheel and follow their dispirited comrades, were the cavalrymen, whose object it had been to smash Perth's right flank.

A trumpet call, a sudden change of formation, the riders wheeling into one long line and then the merry swish of the drawing sword and Daveril's cry.

"Scotland and Prince Charles!"

It seemed as though the horses understood without need of loosened reins or frantic spur, for with bent heads, with hoofs steady and speeding over the even ground, they answered to the order to attack, and like one horse the line tore forward to crash into Cumberland's cavalry.

There was no escape.

Perth's men were tearing forward. They had cast their muskets aside and the gleaming claymores were biting into their foes, for, bunched up in their advance, fancying Perth's force an easy prey, the cavalry now found that retreat was a slower matter than they had fancied, and into their ranks came the screaming, shouting Highlanders, and claymore and sabre echoed together in grim contest.

The troops, attacked by Sir John's men, rolled back on to the wing of Perth's advancing soldiers and then rebounded, to be dashed back again.

Fiona found herself detached from Alastair. A dragoon towered up in front of her, his sabre was raised and had swung round for a slicing cut, but Fiona met the cut with her sword, and felt as though her arm had been broken in the impact.

The dragoon reined in, and now he raised his sabre for a downward stroke, but it never came.

Grim-lipped figures were rushing through the smoke. Perth's men, breaking ranks, were in at the dismayed cavalry, and a great, bearded Highlander had leapt behind the dragoon and, as he caught the descending arm with one firm grip, his claymore cut deep into the cavalryman, who toppled from his horse with an amazed look in his fast-fading eyes.

The man saw Fiona's bonnet and smiled a great smile, and the next moment was gone—gone on his adversary's horse and screaming into the fight, all red-eyed and with a great claymore whistling through the air as he rode.

The fight had raged away. Cumberland's cavalry were in full flight, and Perth's happy warriors were returning to their old position—the road.

And along the road the retreat continued—flowing on and on, with Cumberland between them and the border.

What would be the outcome of the next few hours? If it was to fight, that was the desire of every Highland heart now that they had whetted their claymores and had won initial success.

CHAPTER XXXII

ON CLIFTON MOOR

THE news that Cumberland was cutting the line of retreat had fortunately turned out to be untrue, but he was coming up hard on the heels of the retreating army, and that whole day Alastair and Fiona were engaged with various bodies of cavalry that did their best to capture Murray's wagons.

That they failed in this object was due to the wonderful doggedness of Alastair's kinsmen.

Time and again Cumberland's cavalry charged them, but each time they withdrew with their wounded and their dead, finding the solid wall of Scottish swords too much of a barrier to allow of easy penetration.

No sooner had the cavalry been driven off than the rear guard fell back on the wagons, and there waited for a further charge, and so the day waned on.

Cumberland was having decidedly the worst of the exchange of blows. Murray's force had reached Clifton at last, and here, two miles from Penrith, he determined to do his best to check Cumberland's progress.

Well did Murray know that no less than four thousand men were at his heels, but he felt confident that he could stem this force what time he sent Colonel Roy Stuart to Penrith for reinforcements.

As Stuart cantered out of Clifton village it was to see Murray's men already preparing to meet Cumberland's attack.

If his chief was confident in success, Stuart's views were different, for the Macdonalds had been fighting hammer-and-tongs all day and would be but a poor match for Cumberland's new troops, that were being flung into the fight as soon as they arrived on the scene of battle.

Sir John, pessimistic as to the outcome of the fight, had begged Fiona to ride with Stuart, and, after a deal of persuading, she had consented to do so.

Meanwhile, Cumberland had dismounted five hundred of his cavalry, which were being thrown at Murray's small force, but if he hoped to shake the tired rearguard with this force he was bitterly mistaken.

The order had been given to his concealed men to break through the hedge that protected them and attack the dismounted cavalrymen for all they knew, the object being to drive them back on their main body.

With as little noise as possible the Highlanders cut through the hedges and arrived in the open, to find that the dismounted dragoons were already there and that another hedge reared itself behind their assailants.

With the calm precision of the parade-ground Murray's valiant force gave their fire at the cavalrymen, and then, seeing that the discharge had caused confusion and that their foes had turned their backs and were scurrying for safety, they tore across the open space with a yell that would have awakened the dead.

Above these cries now there sounded the clash of claymore on the helms of the cavalrymen. Claymores sparkled in the night and broke on the steel caps of Cumberland's dismounted men and, driven back against the hedge, they died by it and beneath it.

Cumberland realised full well that scant mercy had been shown to his five hundred men, who were now coming back helter-skelter with the devils of hell at their heels.

In the night a small force can appear to be a very large one, and the force Lord George Murray commanded had assumed enormous proportions in the eyes of Cumberland.

Cumberland meant to retreat and to extricate his discomfited cavalrymen, so, in order to make things uncomfortable for Murray's victory-flushed Highlanders, he sent a further party against Murray's flank and rear, hoping to force his antagonist back on Clifton and get him on the run again.

But the Glengarry men, from the opposite side of the Clifton road, and obeying instructions as to the protection of the flank, were ready and waiting for this movement, and a tremendous and steady fire met this second attack and shattered it.

The survivors beat a hasty retreat with Lord George Murray and his Macphersons in full cry after the whole of the attacking force. Cumberland, indeed, fancied his star had shone for the last time.

In the night regular formations had been sadly broken. The dismounted dragoons in some cases were holding individual combats among themselves, not knowing that they fought with friends.

After the fight by the hedge Alastair had gone off with a party of Macdonalds and the fight had raged several fields away. Then there had come a figure looming up through the mists of darkness, and the next thing that Alastair knew was that he was engaged with a fight-maddened soldier whose eyes shone grimly as he glared at his youthful opponent.

"So, my young blade," he said, "you would fight with His Majesty's dragoons, would you?"

Alastair parried and smiled.

The man glared again, and cut viciously at Alastair, who sprang aside and retorted with a curving blow that just missed the fellow's shoulder.

"*Peste!*" exclaimed the man. "But you fight well, my young blade!"

"Yield!" said Alastair, "and I promise you mercy."

The trooper laughed.

"John Brown yield?" he exclaimed. "Gadzooks, young gentleman, but do you think that John Brown is going to yield to a mere lad?"

"Have at you, then," said Alastair, and he beat down upon John Brown with all the skill he could command.

Alastair could see at once that the man was a consummate swordsman, for he parried and cut with ease, and Alastair felt that he was being played with.

Brown came again at Alastair, and now his blows rained one after the other upon Alastair's claymore.

Macdonald was forced to hop here, there and everywhere to avoid the strokes, and now the lad was panting and sorely spent.

There was almost a look of sorrow in Brown's eyes as he looked at his youthful antagonist.

Poor Alastair was at his wit's end. That John Brown was

his master he knew, and that John Brown was playing with him he also knew, but what he wasn't sure about was defeat, so he fought on until John Brown laid him low with a neat cut that simply stunned Alastair as he raised his target to take the stroke.

Brown had hit full and true on the boss and Alastair went down with the impact of the blow and lay in the grass of Clifton Moor, as the fight roared back to the road and then forward, and swayed to and fro from darkness to the dawn, when Cumberland withdrew and Murray did likewise. Murray knew that he had won a really decisive victory, for he had saved the whole of the retreating army, with the loss of but few, after having inflicted grave casualties on Cumberland's dismounted cavalry.

As for Alastair!

He came to with a terrific pain in his head and a feeling that he was stiff all over.

Opening his eyes, he found there was a faint light coming through the roof above him. Also he discovered that he was bound hand and foot.

Brown had evidently given him a slight wound and had then made him a prisoner.

That it was merciful Alastair knew full well, but that it was decidedly disappointing to be out of further fighting, and humbling to have been brought so low, rather spoilt the first feeling.

Where was he?

He rolled over, and tried to crawl, but found it impossible, so he turned over on his back and looked upwards at the light, and then he saw . . .

An eye was looking down at him.

It wasn't John Brown's eye, for Alastair would never forget that. He could see it now when he closed his own and recalled the fight on the moor.

The eye was the eye of a girl. There was no doubt about that, for a woman's exclamation, unmistakable, had confirmed the fact.

Suddenly he heard a scuffle on the roof above him, the sound of a figure sliding down to the ground, and then the clumping of riding boots and the creak of the opening door.

The light shone on his eyes.

He saw Trooper John Brown standing enshrined in the opening of the hut.

"Well, my lad," said the trooper, "you'll be fit to travel soon. The village is in our hands now and Lord George is hard on the tracks of the rebel prince. You have an almighty amount of courage for a lad of your size. But I'm not discouraging it. I have captured men before, mainly Frenchmen, but they have never been as game as you are. It is almost a pity to take you."

John Brown had barely finished speaking when there came a girlish laugh behind him, and Alastair saw the chambermaid standing by the soldier.

"Well, I never, Mr. Brown," she said. "If this isn't your prisoner! But he's a mere boy!"

Brown threw his chest out.

"He fought me like a man, at any rate," he said.

The girl came nearer to the trooper.

"They sent me with a message to you," she said. "Sergeant Holyoak has an important commission . . ."

"Look after the lad; I shall be but a second," said the trooper, and with that he hurried away.

The next moment the girl was in the hut, and from her stocking she had drawn a knife and was severing Alastair's bonds.

"Hasten away!" she whispered. "I saw you yesterday, and all my thoughts are for your cause. Tell them that the Duke marches on Carlisle."

"How will *you* explain?" asked Alastair. "They may try you for helping a rebel to escape."

"When you are gone," she whispered, "I shall be found here in a swoon, and when they bring me to consciousness I shall say you struck me down—trust me to act the part," she exclaimed. "And now, begone . . ."

Alastair stole from the hut and, glancing behind him, he saw the girl plunge a knife into her shoulder and heard her half-stifled cry, and in his heart the lad vowed to repay that debt.

CHAPTER XXXIII

IN THE GARDEN OF LOCHAVON

BONNIE PRINCE CHARLIE'S army had gained Glasgow, and had fruitlessly attacked Stirling, and whilst the army was so engaged fresh trouble was banking up behind them.

After the failure of Cope, General Hawley had been deputed to take command of the King's forces in Scotland —a much scattered force, but, from Hawley's point of view, sufficient to put Prince Charlie's "bare-legged Scots" to the run.

Hawley's second-in-command was a General named Husk, and it was rumoured that Husk possessed the brains and the bravery of a really capable leader.

Whilst the fruitless attempt to capture Stirling was in progress Alastair, laid low by old wounds, had been given permission to repair to Lochavon with his father.

Thus, whilst a few cannon did their best to demolish the solid defences of Stirling, a party of three rode away on their journey to Lochavon, and at evening time they reached the old and picturesque spot.

Lochavon House was set on a slight eminence overlooking the loch itself, and behind the house the pine trees and firs dreamed away into the distance—and the mountains.

When Alastair had last seen Lochavon the sun was splintering its warm rays through the green trees and the birds were carolling a happy song; but now . . .

The trees were bare; the January snow lay deep over field

and hill, and there was a thick coating of ice on the waters of the loch.

They were nearing the entrance to Lochavon House now, and through the shadows of the early falling night there glowed the light of a lantern.

It was held by an old and trembling hand, and as they came within the radius of its radiance they could see old Kenneth standing by the open door.

"Welcome back to Lochavon!" he said. "It's been weary waiting for ye."

Hamish dismounted and, with both hands outstretched, approached his old kinsman.

"But we are home at last," he said softly, "and I owe it to you, Kenneth, that I have been preserved for this moment."

Kenneth placed his lantern in the snow on the step, and in silence the two men shook hands and then Hamish walked into his house.

Things had changed indeed since he had been there last. The heather had burned to the edge of the moor, and the spying vultures had been found out and had flown. He looked about him and breathed with relief. True, things were different, but they were better.

Hamish walked into the big reception room where already a bright fire had given warmth to the place. News of their coming had been sent on ahead by a messenger travelling north, and Kenneth had prepared for their coming.

That night there was a strange silence in that echoing old room.

Even Fiona, so cheerful generally and so care-free, seemed to want to be alone with her thoughts, and it was the same with Alastair and his father.

They retired early, and, as they slept, away on distant roads men were marching.

The drum and the pipe, the cry of war seemed very far distant but they did not know of armies moving into action.

of marching and counter-marching, the play for the opening, the choice of the best position.

The astute brains of Prince Charlie's command were working as they had never worked before. Lord George was leading the now concentrated army across the Carron at Dunipace, and in the crossing Hawley's army came in view.

Lord John Drummond, making a feint of advancing by the north side of the Torwood, had deceived the King's army into the belief that from this point would come the main attack, and that this was the main body.

They formed in battle order to meet him, and felt secure in the lack of action on the part of their foes, for on the distant road they had seen a party of Highlanders retiring on Stirling, and the sight of the broad banner of the Stuart floating from the headquarters on Plean Moor further mystified Hawley and suggested that the Stuart forces did not mean serious business.

The blustering wind was rising in intensity, and now the great black banks of snowcloud rolled up into the heavens, to darken the vision and to send down the first harbingers of the storm.

White flakes began to blot out the countryside and through the mantle of them, white-lipped and with frightened eyes, came a man.

"To arms!" he shouted. "They are upon us—coming along the road from the south-west and in all their force. The Highlanders!"

Had a bomb exploded beneath the feet of General Husk he could not have been more greatly surprised.

It was evil fortune for him that the gallant Commander-in-Chief, General Hawley, should be lunching at Callander House with the Countess of Kilmarnock, and it is to be feared that General Husk's misfortune was not dissevered from the good fortune of the courteous Countess, who was so charming in her wit and so excellent as a hostess that she took gallant Hawley away from his task of defeating the "bare-legged Scots."

On that day General Hawley was outmanœuvred by the skill of a woman who was a staunch Jacobite, and she must have laughed when the gallant General, warned of impending battle, dashed to his horse and, hatless, rode like the wind for Falkirk.

Hawley was in no mood for battle. His temper had got the better of him, and he was so blind with rage that quick commands were as quickly cancelled, and out of the confusion only the skeleton of a plan was conceived.

With cool precision Murray's men waited. They held their fire until the dragoons, under Whitney, came well within range, and then the line fired as one man and down came those horsemen in wounds and confusion.

The volley had worked a more deadly effect than wounds amongst Whitney's men. They wheeled and, heedless of the disaster they were causing, rode down on the infantry who were supporting their charge.

But there were among Whitney's men those who did not show the white feather. They thundered into the ranks of the Highlanders and cut and slashed their way amongst them. Trampling many a defender down, sabring the tumbling Highlander.

But the Highlanders took swift vengeance for this small setback. Leaping at the dragoons they engaged them in single combat, or dirked the horses.

Some of the cavalrymen were pulled from their horses by means of the long tails of their coats or by their legs. The dragoons were having the worst of the tussle, and those who could withdrew.

Meanwhile the Macdonalds, ever impetuous, seeing the cavalry broken and the infantry in disorder, broke their line and charged madly upon their late opponents, driving them pell-mell into the support that had failed them.

One English foot regiment stood their ground, however,

and so effectually checked the onrush of the Highlanders that the day was saved from being a disaster.

By nightfall General Hawley was in full retreat on Edinburgh, having burned his tents behind him, and on his flanks the clansmen hovered like vultures over a field of war.

At Lochavon the sighing wind that had brought the snow carried no news of the happenings at Falkirk, nor did Alastair have the slightest thought that battle had been joined, for, when he had left Plean Moor, Hawley was not expected to make any serious attempt to attack.

For him the short winter day held another interest.

Fiona and he had wandered to a spot that had always been connected with their childhood.

It was known as the Wishing Stone and was a large black rock that perched above the loch and beneath a gaunt tree.

"Let us sit on the stone, Fiona," said Alastair. "It will be quite like the past. Do you remember?"

Fiona laughed.

"I should think I do!" she said. "If it had not been for you, Alastair, I should not be here to tell the story to-day."

"Do *you* remember?" she added, "how I slipped and fell and you dived in and saved me?"

Alastair smiled.

"If Kenneth had not come along with the boat I should have gone down with you," he said quietly. "Kenneth saved you."

Fiona linked her arm through her cousin's.

"No!" she whispered. "It was you, Alastair."

"Somehow," she murmured, "you have always protected me ever since I can remember."

Alastair looked deep into her eyes.

"And now," he said slowly, "I want to protect you always, Fiona."

"I have wanted to speak before," he added, "but the time was not right."

Fiona's eyes were like stars as she looked up.

"I am glad you have spoken," she said. "I knew what

you knew, Alastair, for how was it possible that either of us should be ignorant of our love?"

Alastair bent and kissed her, and then, and in a silence more eloquent than words, they wandered back to where Lochavon stood out against her background of pines.

CHAPTER XXXIV

THE GALLOWS

"AYE!" exclaimed General Hawley. "I brought them to hang rebels with, but now there are no rebels they shall serve a better purpose."

His eyes were red with anger, his brows were knit, and his pugnacious face was wreathed into so many creases that he looked twice his age.

A great, red fist came down on the oaken table of the farmhouse, so that it rattled the pewter on the dresser against the wall.

General Husk surveyed his chief with tolerance, but some of the officers in the room looked nervously at their commander-in-chief and some were obviously alarmed.

"Aye!" shouted Hawley again. "A cowardly lot of skunks!"

And outside in the snow, towering above the road along which weary troops were marching, some gallows raised themselves.

Hawley, sure of defeating Bonnie Prince Charlie's force, had had these gallows constructed for the purpose of hanging the Stuart supporters, but as yet no good Jacobite heads had dangled from the beam.

"Who was the officer, Husk . . . ?" he thundered. "I'll hang the officer and every man of his squadron. Who was he?"

Hawley glowered around him, so that the officers clustered by the door looked fearful and sought to get away from his eyes.

He stormed at them.

"A pretty lot, all of you!" he shouted. "Brave in uniform —but on the field, oh, my God, what a sight you presented! They broke you like chaff. Do you think I'm Cope, or what? Do you think I'll have the name of Hawley made the laughing-stock of the army? Men! . . ."

Husk looked grave.

"The squadron was Lieutenant Harding's," he said abruptly. "Harding's officer had been killed by a stray ball, so the Lieutenant took command."

"Where is the skunk?"

Hawley turned towards the door, to see that no one slipped out.

"He is not here, sir," said Husk quietly. "He volunteered for a private commission. The Lieutenant said he knew of big Stuart funds concealed in a mansion."

"I have never had much opinion of the Lieutenant's bravery or his brilliance as a cavalry leader, so I thought him more useful on this mission."

"You seem mighty considerate for the fellow's health!" scoffed Hawley.

"His father was General Harding, sir . . ."

Hawley now thumped both his fists on the table until it nearly cracked.

"I don't care if his father was the King of England!" he raved. "He ran away in front of the enemy . . ."

"Let me know the moment Harding returns," said Hawley sharply. "And now to horse!"

Husk followed, and many a trembling officer stumped out behind him.

.   .   .   .

Alastair and Fiona had told their secret to Hamish Macdonald, and had received his blessing, and now, on the spot where they had plighted their troth, they were discussing the future.

"I feel I must get back to the army," said Alastair. "You will stay here now, Fiona, as I could not bear to see you in danger. And I feel that my father has gone through so much that he needs a woman's attention."

Fiona looked sad.

"It will be dreadful to part with you, Alastair," she whispered. "But I would not keep you at my side when your sword is needed with our Prince."

"What was that . . . ?"

She looked up suddenly, and then turned to Alastair.

Neither spoke, but both listened intently, and then, ever so faintly in the distance, there came the sound of jangling harness.

"Riders on the Lochavon Road."

Alastair rose to his feet as he spoke.

And now the merry music of horse hoofs came to them distinctly, and the jangle of harness sounded like little bells calling across the snow.

"Let us get to the fringe of the trees," said Fiona quickly. "We can scan the road from there."

She lowered herself from the rock, and the two hurried across the ice to the far edge of the loch, and then through the fir trees.

They were on an eminence, and beyond them a clear view of the road could be obtained.

"There they are!" exclaimed Alastair suddenly, gripping Fiona's arm and pointing with his left hand to where some trotting figures turned a bend in the road.

Fiona gasped.

"Red coats!" she said, her face growing pale. "Dragoons, Alastair, and coming this way!"

"Come," he cried. "We must get back to the house, and ride off with my father and Kenneth."

Skirting the loch they ran as though dear life depended on it, and they were out of breath by the time the house came to view.

Fiona ran into the hall followed by Alastair just as the

door of the reception room opened and the white face of old Kenneth appeared in the opening.

"The chief!" he whispered. "The chief!"

Kenneth pointed a trembling finger in the direction of the room from whence he had come.

"In there" he said weakly, "on the floor."

With a cry, Alastair brushed the dazed old man aside and ran into the room.

Hamish Macdonald, livid of face and his hands gripped in a grim convulsion, lay on his back with his eyes staring at the ceiling.

Alastair knelt at his side.

"Father!" he said hoarsely. "Father, what is it?"

But Hamish did not speak. That he was alive the boy could see, for the lips were trying to speak, but could not, and there was consciousness in the staring eyes.

Alastair looked hopelessly at Fiona, who had come to his side.

"What shall we do?" he asked. "He has been struck down by something and we cannot leave him, Fiona."

Fiona's lips had tightened. Her eyes were two points of flame.

"They shall not take you, Alastair!" she cried.

"You mean fight them, Fiona?" he said quickly.

"Aye," she answered. "And to the death! Let us bear the Chief above and then prepare."

It was a difficult job, but at last Hamish Macdonald was carried upstairs and put to bed, with Kenneth to watch him, and as Fiona and Alastair ran below, the sound of knocking came upon the oaken outer door.

Fiona looked at Alastair.

"It cannot be the dragoons?" she said.

"See who it is, Fiona, whilst I get the muskets," said Alastair.

Three men stood on the threshold. They were old men, too infirm to go with Charlie, but not too infirm to strike a blow at home for his cause.

"Soldiers on the lower road to Lochavon!" gasped one. "We came, Miss Macdonald; Dougald and Roy here have their muskets, but I am without arms."

Alastair, with an armful of muskets, powder, shot and swords had come from the little armoury and he took in the situation at a glance.

"Dougald, Roy and Allan!" he cried. "You knew we were here?"

"We had the news from Kenneth," said Dougald, "and when we saw the soldiers . . ." he paused. "We heard talk of hanging, so we came," he added, with grim lips.

"We must barricade the windows," said Alastair, "and the door—you two, Dougald and Allan, take the front rooms; Roy and I will see that the back is secure. There is an iron door there. The whole place is strong."

They worked like furies to get the house into a state of defence. Heavy furniture was dragged to the windows and bedding cast over it, and the front door was doubly secured by the help of beams and furniture.

The defenders then hurried to the upper windows, just in time to see a squadron of dragoons riding up the avenue, and at their head rode an unmistakable figure.

The sound of jangling horse-bits and clanking sabres came noisily to the ears as Harding led his troop towards the house.

Never very sound in strategy, he came just a trifle too close, for, before he knew what was happening, two puffs of smoke had followed two reports, and one of his men pitched from his saddle into the snow, whilst another gripped his arm in agony and reeled unsteadily.

Saul Harding looked up at the windows just as Roy Macdonald let fly a shot at him, which, although missing the Lieutenant, laid a horse low.

"Back to cover," cried Harding, and, suiting the action to the word, he rode out of range and took in the situation.

This sudden check was decidedly discomfiting.

The snow was beginning to fall again, and it was soon

so thick that the cloaks they had hastily donned were white mantles.

"They won't attack until the night," said Alastair. "See, they are surrounding the house."

Parties of dragoons were now skirting the house and taking up positions on all sides of it. They made no attempt at attack, and the day became a grim wait for what might happen, but nothing did happen save the occasional relieving of sentries.

The day waned to its close. The snowstorm was still raging, and the darkness came sooner than natural, having the assistance of a gloomy and overcast sky.

The wind howled mournfully through the firs and pine trees. It must have been a cold vigil for Harding's soldiers.

Alastair viewed the approach of night with apprehension. There were at least fifty dragoons, the odds were ten to one, and three of the defending party were infirm and useless if it came to close quarters.

Suddenly, glancing down, Alastair saw cloaked figures carrying some long object, running at the door.

He fired into the mass and heard a cry, and in the dimness saw a man drop, but the others, leaving him in the snow, ran on with their battering-ram, for now Alastair could see, as he hastily reloaded his piece, that they bore a small tree with them.

Leaning over he fired again—just as the tree thudded into the stout panels of the door.

"Watch here, and fire as fast as you can," said Alastair to Fiona. "Take the pistols, for they are all loaded and the range is good. I'll get to the stairs in case they reach the hall."

Snatching up a claymore, Alastair ran from the chamber and so came to the stairs to hear the sound of shots intermingled with the crashing of the ram.

The door was giving!

One panel had crashed in, and the tree showed through it.

Then the tree was withdrawn, and a face appeared in the opening the ram had made.

Alastair fired, and had the satisfaction of hearing a scream, and he saw a hand come up to an agonised face.

Grimly he reloaded and waited. Another panel was shattered and then the door fell inwards and a rush of figures stormed against the furniture that bolstered up the door.

They swept it aside in their onrush, and now Dougald, Allan and Fiona had joined Alastair and the firing became heavier. They did much damage among the crowded mass that sought to win the stairs.

Once they swept them back, but again the dragoons came forward, and now they were up the stairs. Dougald and Allan were down with musket ball wounds, and Fiona and Alastair stood alone. Alastair was winged, but he remained fighting at her side and, white-faced and grim, they waited for the inevitable.

More dragoons were in the hall, and now Alastair discovered that his ammunition had run out. "Get above!" he said to Fiona. "I stay here."

As he spoke Harding's men made their last rush and, as they did so, from without Lochavon House, carried over on the wind, there came a blood-curdling scream, as though a thousand furies were rushing to the rescue.

Alastair reeled amid a ring of glittering sabres.

CHAPTER XXXV

THE COMING OF THE MACDONALDS

ALASTAIR fought on with a mist of steel before his eyes. He could see nothing else, there was not even time to glance to where Fiona stood. She had disobeyed his command, and was assisting in the defence as best she could.

But now, above the clash of swords, carried nearer and

nearer on the icy winter wind, there came that scream through the night and the rush of feet and a whirling, hacking mass of men were in the hall. They had come in a flash, and Harding's dragoons had had no time to make their escape.

All Alastair knew was that suddenly and as if by magic that wall of steel in front of him had melted away, and he was standing fascinated at the sight below him.

Whirling claymores were playing havoc with a tiny force of surviving dragoons who had huddled themselves into a corner for safety, and safer they found it, for their officer, having no stomach for odds of this sort, was begging for mercy from a great, gaunt Highlander with a cut down his cheek and a flaming mop of hair that sought to rival the tint on his face.

"' Red Angus '!"

The cry came from Alastair, and now he was down in the hall and gripping the Macdonald's hand whilst "Red's" clansmen led the survivors of the fight out into the snow.

"Only just in time!" said Angus. "We heard dragoons were here—Dougald's wife met us on the lower road."

"But what were you doing there?" asked Alastair.

Angus Macdonald smiled.

"We have fought at Falkirk," he said, "and we have broken Hawley's army—he is in retreat, and all night we have been hanging on his flanks; but his men went too fast for us."

Alastair laughed. He could afford to do so now. Now when victory had come and they had been saved from the hands of their foes and the malice of Saul Harding. Alastair spoke to Angus of his step-brother.

"Harding shall have scant mercy," said Macdonald grimly.

Alastair laid his hand on the Highlander's shoulder.

"Not that, ' Red,'" he said. "Goodness knows I have no love for him, but we can afford to be magnanimous now, and maybe it might teach him a lesson. We cannot take prisoners, as you know. Give them their horses and let them go, they have suffered enough and they are but few. The others . . ."

Alastair looked at the shambled figures lying on the floor of Lochavon's hall.

Macdonald nodded.

"It would have done him good to have tasted the rope," he said gruffly. "But your view is the best after all. So far we have not disgraced our cause."

"Red Angus" stamped out into the snow, and Alastair heard him giving the order to free the dragoons and send them on the road to Hawley's retreating army.

Then Alastair turned, for the sound of quiet sobbing had come to his ears. He looked towards the stairs to see Dougald supporting Fiona.

With a cry Alastair ran up the stairs.

Fiona clenched her teeth. "It's the shoulder, Alastair," she murmured. "A sabre cut only . . ."

The next moment she collapsed in Dougald's arms.

"It is but a slight wound," said Dougald. "A few days and she will be well again."

Alastair breathed with relief, and whilst Dougald tended Allan, who had also got a slight wound, he bore Fiona above and bound her shoulder and brought her back to consciousness.

He watched over her until she slept, and then slipped away to see his father. Kenneth was by his kinsman's side, and it was apparent that Hamish Macdonald was better.

He smiled as Alastair came to his side.

"It was the fatigue of the journey, Alastair," he said. "I shall be all right soon. What a storm it has been! It sounded as though the air was full of human voices."

Alastair smiled. He did not tell his father of the grim fight on the stairs, or how rescue had come at the eleventh hour.

"Take care of him, Kenneth," he cautioned the old man. "I must leave Lochavon to-night to rejoin the army."

He bade his father farewell and then went below and wrote a short note to Fiona.

When he laid it by her side she was still sleeping, nor did she wake as he bent over her and kissed her hair; and then he was gone, to join "Red Angus" and his men, who were chafing at the inaction.

The night and the snow closed over a party of High-landers who were returned to join the Prince's army.

.   .   .   .

And through the night and the snow rode a party of dragoons bent on finding Hawley, and find his army they did.

Cantering along the snow-covered road they came upon his vedettes and at last the distant bivouac, and then they fell in with a troop upon the road.

Saul Harding saluted the leader of the troop.

It was General Husk, and the troop was partly composed of his staff.

General Husk recognised the officer despite the falling snow, and his look was hard.

"Place this officer under arrest!" he said grimly.

"But, sir . . ." exclaimed Harding.

Husk did not speak again.

Two officers had ridden to either side of Saul and he had been deprived of his sword.

General Husk cantered off, followed by the two officers and their prisoner, and some ten minutes later Harding was facing Hawley.

Hawley was sharp and to the point.

"You have neglected your military duties; you have shown fear in the face of the enemy; you have been partly responsible for a set-back to the army. There is only one punishment for your crime, Lieutenant."

Hawley pointed a steady finger to the window and what towered ominously above the snowy road.

"The gallows . . ." It was not an exclamation so much as

a frightened cry that Harding gave, and he sought to break away from his guard, but they held him fast.

"Take the man away!" shouted Hawley.

And Saul was taken away.

CHAPTER XXXVI

STIRLING—AND AFTER

THE siege of Stirling Castle dragged on, until at last, sensible of the deep sincerity of his leaders' opinions, Prince Charles Edward was compelled to raise it.

By the beginning of February the army was in retreat to Inverness, and the retreat began to prove more successful than the retreat from England had been. Additional recruits flocked to the standard of the Prince as the three divisions took their separate roads northwards.

Alastair Macdonald rode with the Prince's staff along the military road, and he was glad to find that Sir John Daveril, instead of travelling with Lord George Murray, had been transferred to the Prince's staff.

They were all heartily glad to be on the move again, after the fruitless task of besieging Stirling Castle.

Alastair's adventures were few. True, when Prince Charlie advanced upon Inverness Loudoun retreated before him, and Fort Augustus fell and Fort William didn't; but the fighting was of a somewhat fruitless nature and Alastair was not called upon for any particular show of service.

These various expeditions were weakening the food resources of the army and through them the army was growing smaller each day.

Sir John Daveril eyed the future with no great optimism.

"If only we could fight whilst we have an army to fight with," he said gloomily. "These marches and counter-marches only sap the spirit of the best troops we have—the clansmen—and they do not bring off any *coup* of military importance.

But Sir John was soon to have his wish—soon the grey dawn was to rise on another field, and to that field Cumberland was marching.

High spirits were returning to the army at the thought of battle, and the pipes were played and the drums beat, and Bonnie Prince Charlie's men met him with encouraging shouts as he rode through their lines.

"We'll give Cumberland another Fontenoy!"

And Cumberland marched on.

CHAPTER XXXVII

CULLODEN

"When in deep Glenfinnan's valley
　　Thousands on their bended knees
Saw once more that stately ensign
　　Waving in the northern breeze.
When the noble Tullibardine
　　Stood beneath its weltering fold
With the Ruddy Lion ramping
　　In its field of treasured gold!
When the mighty heart of Scotland,
　　All too big to slumber more,
Burst in wrath and exultation,
　　Like a huge volcano's roar!
There they stand, the battered columns
　　Underneath the murky sky
In the hush of desperation,
　　Not to conquer *but to die.*"

GAY pipes playing to the northern breeze and the tapping of drums. The loud cries of marching men and the spring of hope alike in heart and air.

On through the streets of Inverness towards the chosen ground—bound for the field without Culloden House, where fates were to be decided and a page of gallant history writ with the blood of brave men.

All through the day marching men. The Duke of Perth from Speyside, Lord George Murray to a night attack on Nairn, and the van of the army in movement to Drummossie Muir near to Culloden.

And Cumberland?

Fearful of a Fontenoy, wary and watchful, and with artillery—and food.

Alas! fortune fed the army of Joshua with manna from the sky, but there was no such providential aid to stouten the bodies of Charlie's men.

The Prince himself had but bread and a drink, and his men only a small loaf each which was almost uneatable.

But not a murmur. Craving for food they looked upon as a meanness of the flesh when there lay something so great within their souls.

It seemed that, despite Bonnie Prince Charlie's belief in victory, despite the spirit with which he had inspired his troops, events were working against him.

Counsels had gone disregarded. O'Sullivan, the Prince's adjutant, would not be moved from his view that the moor was a splendid position, whereas it was by no means suited to Highland forms of fighting.

But Lord George Murray's advice was set at nought, and, to add to the disastrous plans, the Macdonalds had been deprived of their traditional position on the field of battle. They had suffered loyally, they had stood by their Prince, and in the great moment they had waited for, they were being slighted before the whole army.

"Red Angus" cut at the heather with his claymore.

"The line will never move," he said. "Here on the left there will be neither retreat nor advance. The men will not stir, for an insult sinks deep into a Highland heart."

Alastair had asked permission to fight with his clan, and now, as he looked at the men near to him, saw the rage in their eyes, he knew that if once they had set themselves to do a certain thing not even the fear of death would alter that purpose.

At one o'clock, with each army in two lines, and with Cumberland's army of ten thousand men facing Prince Charlie's force of five thousand, the issue was joined.

The artillery opened the battle, but the Highland pieces were but poorly served against artillery that was being aimed truly and fired under the direction of a notable officer.

Cumberland's cannonade was doing a work of devastation amongst the ranks of the impatient clansmen.

Men cannot stand idly waiting for death when open ground lies between them and the enemy, but the heroism and the discipline of those gaunt men was so fine that they stood their ground whilst their comrades went down to right and left of them.

"Oh, why don't we charge?" almost sobbed "Red Angus." "Are we to be killed before a blow is struck for Scotland?"

At last the clamorous voice of reason rose from all parts of the Scottish line.

"Lead us against them!" they cried.

Prince Charles had sent an aide-de-camp to order a general advance, but the rider was killed, and, before Lord George Murray himself could order the attack, the Macintosh clan, stung to fury by the effect of the artillery, broke their position and rushed to attack the enemy.

And now the line was moving forward. Stuarts, Frasers, Camerons and the M'Cleans dashed towards the guns regardless that they were being fired at point-blank range. Despite terrible losses they got amidst the guns, nor did they waver from a musket volley from the infantry behind.

They broke in on the regiments sword in hand, and now the scream of their war-cry rose above the field.

Cumberland's men fought well and hard, but the onrush had been too fierce and a whole regiment was annihilated by the dash of the Camerons and the Frasers.

With the utmost gallantry they swarmed against Cumberland's second line. But these regiments held their fire until the range was certain to be effective and then they gave it. The clansmen withered away into scattered groups, and these went on to pierce themselves upon the bayonets of Sempill's soldiery.

On Prince Charlie's left the Macdonalds had kept their vow. They stood as though rooted to the spot, with their hungry, furious eyes on the ground. With their claymores they slashed at the heather, but they would not move.

The Duke of Perth begged, stormed, but they would not move.

Since the days of Bannockburn they had fought on Scotland's right and the same should have been to-day.

But one man there forgot the insult. It was the gallant Keppoch, who, claymore in hand and alone, advanced against the foe.

"My God! have the children of my tribe forsaken me?" he cried.

Alastair watched him go. It was more than he could bear.

With claymore flashing he dashed after Keppoch, and caught the chieftain as he fell with a bullet in his chest.

"Come back!" cried Alastair to him. "Come back, Keppoch!"

"No!" answered Keppoch. "It is on—ever on!"

He staggered to his feet and charged against the silent hosts in front of him and fell riddled with bullets, and he rose no more.

Alastair cast a despairing glance at Keppoch, and then seeing that the Macdonalds were falling back, he moved towards the right wing and found himself near to Prince Charles.

They were breaking. The Prince could see that, and Alastair could see it too.

What remained of some of the clans were retreating in the direction of Badenoch, and the Frasers and the Irish legion were falling back on Inverness, with Cumberland's dragoons at their heels.

The day was lost, and massacre had begun. The road to Inverness was a tragic enough sight. Those gay fighters that had marched down it towards the moor now lay stark and stiff, huddled in ditches or lying in the path of the tramping horses.

Alastair had helped to fend off a wing attack by cavalry, and had been fortunate enough to find a horse.

With Sir John Daveril repeated charges had been made against advancing infantry, and with a little cavalry covering Prince Charlie, gathering his few trusted friends, rode from the field in the direction of Nairn.

The Bonnie Prince had become a fugitive, and Alastair was a fugitive with him.

CHAPTER XXXVIII

THE FUGITIVE

"ALASTAIR MACDONALD, you have served me with true loyalty."

The man looked up at Alastair Macdonald.

He was still recognisable as the gay young Chevalier who had won the heart of Scotland, but his eyes were tired and his cheeks were pale from want of food, and privations and anxiety had etched little lines below his eyes.

"Your Royal Highness!"

It was all that Alastair could make reply. At present they were lying on two heather beds in a cave in the Western Highlands, and they had lain there for days, depending upon the honour and the charity of neighbouring gentlemen.

But none were safe, for the neighbouring gentlemen had fought with or had sympathised with the Prince, and as day followed day the net round the royal fugitive was being drawn closer and closer.

"We must get away!" said Prince Charles. "It is not safe here. If I could reach Boisdale there might be better safety there, and there are loyal enough friends by the loch."

"Yes, sire," concurred Alastair, "but is it safe to move yet?"

"Why not?" came the quick question.

"I fear for you," came the quiet reply. "One day you will come again; you must be careful now."

A far-away look came into the fugitive's eyes.

"One day I shall come again," he whispered. "I wonder . . ."

He turned over and Alastair saw that he slept, and into that sleep the ghosts of yesterday must have crept, for his lids flickered and spasms of pain seemed to be passing across his face. It was as though Culloden's lonely moor had come before him. It was as though he was watching the sullen Macdonald line, the last death-dash of the Frasers, the fate of the Camerons, and listening to the sullen melody of Cumberland's cannon.

The fugitives moved that night, and stole with all the rapidity they could command in the direction of the sea.

There were hands to help them. By day and by night they were guarded, by day and by night no movement of any of those who searched for Prince Charles went unnoticed and so they came near to the coast.

Weeks and months they travelled. They rowed through the stormy seas to the island of Benbecula, and four days and four nights they lay hidden there in a small hut.

They came within cannon range of a ship-of-war, but Providence saved the prince and brought him at last to Boisdale. But soldiers came to Boisdale, so back to the island the party returned.

From the island to South Uist, and there fate played her trump card.

Alastair had had occasion to travel to Milton for food, and there he had to see Macdonald of South Uist.

Macdonald greeted him somewhat guardedly and Alastair was not a little surprised. He had entered a darkened room, and not until his eyes became accustomed to the light did he see the slim figure of a girl seated in the corner.

She was apparently taking stock of Alastair, but Alastair had almost forgotten about her a few minutes later as he hurried back with the provisions he had obtained.

Macdonald had not gone far enough when he was hailed, and, turning, he saw the girl running after him.

"My brother tells me that you are from the Prince," she murmured. "Oh, tell me, sir, is all well with him?"

Alastair lowered his eyes.

"He is well," he answered, "but he feels this matter terribly and grows pale with the fatigue of it."

The girl, for she was little more, looked worried.

"If I could only help!" she said quickly. "My name is Macdonald, just as yours is, for my brother told me. I am Flora Macdonald."

"Then, Miss Macdonald," said Alastair, "could your woman's wit devise some scheme?"

A rosy flush mantled her cheek.

"I have it," she exclaimed. "I am travelling back to Skye, from whence I came. Why should the Prince not return with me?"

"But how?"

"In the simplest of all disguises," came the ready answer. "As a woman, and as maid to myself."

Alastair's eyes lit up.

"Now," she said hastily, "return and prepare him for my plan and I will not fail you. Be on this road at midnight, and I will have made all my arrangements by then."

Alastair's heart was almost bursting with excitement as he hurried back to their hiding-place and put the scheme to Prince Charles Edward.

"I can vouch for her loyalty," he assured the Prince.

The fugitive thought for a moment and at last he looked up. "Macdonald!" he exclaimed. "It seems a Godsend. We are at our wit's end how to turn. Will she fail us?"

"I am sure she will not, sire?" answered Alastair.

He was at the rendezvous at the stipulated time, and Flora Macdonald was already there, and with her was Lady Clanranald.

"I have arranged everything," said Miss Macdonald. "The prince will come as my maid. I have obtained a passport for myself, a manservant and my maid. So his escape should be a simple matter."

The three wasted no time, but came to the hut where Prince Charles was concealed, and there Flora Macdonald was presented to the Prince and she told him her plan.

They definitely decided to make the attempt, and on the following day Alastair took his leave of Bonnie Prince Charlie. They were standing on the shore of Benbecula, and those who saw Alastair Macdonald bend and kiss the hand of the figure gowned in calico and wearing a hood were the only ones who knew that the garb concealed the ill-starred Chevalier.

"Macdonald!" said Charles Edward with deep sincerity. "If ever I come again I know of one sword that will flash to my service. Your loyalty shall prove an inspiration during my exile. Farewell!"

With that the Prince stepped into the boat in which Flora Macdonald was already seated, with Neil Macdonald and four boatmen, who gave way as Prince Charles took his place. Once he turned and waved to where Alastair stood as though cut out of the rock. And Alastair stood so until the boat was but a speck in the distance.

At last, and with tear-dimmed eyes, he turned back and, weary and sad, made his way across the island.

The hope of Scotland had come and now he had departed for ever. With the help of Flora Macdonald he was destined to escape to France, and in that land the Fates decreed his star should set.

.   .   .   .

Many mists had passed over Culloden's grim moor before Scotia's wounds were healed at last, and many things had happened. Hamish Macdonald had passed away, and Alastair had been treated with clemency by the royal authorities.

The wilds and the wastes had claimed him until freedom was his at last; and all this while a wistful-eyed girl had watched the lower Lochavon road for her lover's return.

One day he came back, came back through the trees, and she saw him coming, and together and as children they walked down to the shore of the loch, now a silvery surface beneath the glory of the sun.

"It has been weary waiting, dearest," she whispered. "But hope never left my breast."

"And love never left mine," he murmured. "Your eyes were with me through the whole vigil, Fiona; but now we need sorrow no more."

She crept into his arms, just as when a child she had come for protection there, and only the trees saw them; and for lovers' music there came the ripple of the loch's clear waters.